E

"So," [illegible]
desk. "Harry was tortured to death."

"Yes," Patreaux whispered. "The teeth marks are human. Eight of his fingers were gone, and there were chunks missing from his stomach, thighs, buttocks and his left calf . . . The doctors who did the autopsy estimate between two-and-a-half and three weeks. Many of the wounds showed signs of partial healing."

"To keep him alive that long, they must have used a torture doctor."

Patreaux reached for the whiskey bottle. "We think so," he answered softly.

Chant lowered his arms, folding his hands in his lap. "What were they trying to find out?"

Patreaux swallowed hard. "I don't think they were trying to find out anything."

Chant pointed to the autopsy report. "Then why . . . that? These people aren't amateurs—not when they use a torture doctor who's probably a trained surgeon. Why keep him alive three weeks doing *that* to him?"

"Punishment," Patreaux said in a haunted voice . . .

Books in the CHANT series from Jove

CHANT
SILENT KILLER

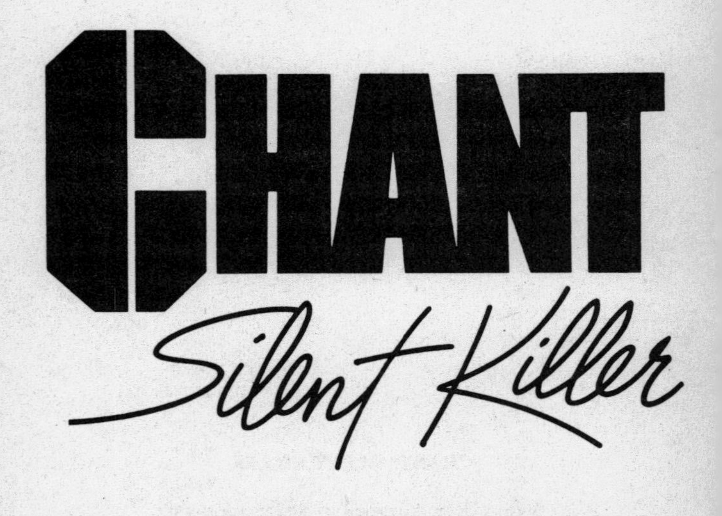

DAVID CROSS

A JOVE BOOK

CHANT: SILENT KILLER

A Jove Book/published by arrangement with
the author

PRINTING HISTORY
Jove edition/July 1986

ISBN: 0-515-08601-0

Jove Books are published by The Berkley Publishing Group,
200 Madison Avenue, New York, N.Y. 10016.

PRINTED IN THE UNITED STATES OF AMERICA

ONE

Something dead and rotting that once might have been human, a loser in Amsterdam's extensive lottery in international crime, floated past him in the canal. The man others called Chant ducked away from the balloon-bloated corpse, then treaded water while he adjusted the straps of the waterproof backpack he wore over his black rubber wet suit. Then he resumed swimming across the wide canal, using a powerful breaststroke that propelled him through the garbage-strewn, midnight water as silently as a tidal ripple from the open sea a half mile away.

When he reached the grease-slick waterline on the stone base of the four-story, wood-frame warehouse that was his target, the man with the iron-colored eyes and hair again treaded water while he unlooped a length of thin nylon rope from around his neck; attached to one end of the rope was a lightweight but strong carbon-alloy steel grappling hook. Supporting himself in the water with a lazy but very powerful scissors kick, he leaned back and began to swing the grappling hook over his head, gradually letting out rope and increasing velocity until the hook whistled just above the surface of the water in a circle that was almost seven feet in diamater. A powerful kick and pull with his left arm raised his body out of the water almost to his waist as he changed the angle of his swing slightly and released the rope. The hook soared up into the night, arced across the face of the full moon, and landed on the roof, clearing a three-foot-high cement cornice.

Chant gently tugged on the rope until the hook caught, then tested the rope with a series of increasingly strong pulls. Finally, satisfied that the hook was securely anchored, he gripped the rope with both his gloved hands, planted his feet against the side of the building, and hauled his six-foot, six-inch body out of the water. Then, with considerable speed and little apparent effort, he "walked" up the side of the building, dropped over the cornice, and pulled the rope up after him.

He stripped off the wet suit and threw it aside, then opened the backpack and took out a set of neatly folded clothes. Within less than a minute he was dressed in a warm black turtleneck sweater, black seaman's cap, black, loose-fitting slacks, and black sneakers. Again he looped the rope and grappling hook around his neck, picked up the backpack, and moved silently across the tarred pebbles of the rooftop, keeping low so as not to be silhouetted against the moon or the garish, neon glow of Amsterdam's night sky. He reached a skylight with dirt-encrusted windows, knelt to examine the ancient, rusted padlock that held the cover in place. Within moments he had picked the lock, opened the cover just wide enough to let his body through, then swung down onto a narrow, railed catwalk that ran around the perimeter of the huge warehouse, just beneath the ceiling. He squatted in the darkness, bracing himself against a steel railing, and studied the activity in the cavernous space below him.

A tractor trailer had been pulled up to the open bay doors of the warehouse, and three of Hugo VanderKlaven's thugs were sweating and cursing as they loaded crates of adulterated antibiotics into the truck. VanderKlaven himself was not there, although he should have been in order to deliver a final payment of a million pounds sterling in exchange for falsified shipping documents, Customs seals and bills of lading, to be delivered by a man VanderKlaven believed to be a corrupt South African official in charge of health services in the black "homelands." In the pharmaceutical mogul's place was a thin, balding man known as Acid because of his propensity for killing his victims—VanderKlaven's enemies—by pouring muriatic acid into their eyes and ears, and down their throats. Acid was standing by himself in an aisle between stacks of crates, sipping dark, Dutch coffee from a ceramic mug. A man dressed in stained workman's clothes whom Chant had never seen before and who Chant assumed was the driver of the truck stood off to one side, smoking a cigarette and looking bored.

So Rolf Bakker, an identity Chant had created for himself with painstaking care, a fictional Afrikaaner he performed in a halting manner with a slight lisp, was to have been killed off instead of paid off this evening, Chant thought with a grim smile. It was a hell of a way for VanderKlaven to do business, and was going to cause Chant some inconvenience—but not a great deal. This operation had been relatively easy and, once it had been set up, not even very time-consuming; the two months he had spent in South Africa researching those strands of VanderKlaven's web of death and corruption, stalking and finally killing the

Dutchman's original Afrikaaner contact and establishing himself as "Rolf Bakker" had been more like a welcome and much-needed vacation than work. Chant, as "Rolf Bakker," had already collected a million pounds sterling as his down payment, and he would visit VanderKlaven at his leisure, at a later date, to collect the rest of his money along with interest that would be the last the obese man with three-piece suits, diamond rings, and death for sale would ever pay.

Chant straightened up and, silent as a great, stalking jungle cat, moved around the catwalk until he was in a position directly over Acid. He draped the straps of the backpack over his left shoulder, took the rope from around his neck, and fashioned the free end into a lasso. Then he leaned out over the railing in the darkness near the ceiling and slowly began to lower the rope, twirling it slightly to keep the lasso loop extended. Finally he let it drop; the loop dropped cleanly over the thin man's balding head, landing with a light slap on the concrete floor. Instantly, Chant yanked on the rope, tightening the loop around the man's ankles, snatching him off his feet and pulling him up into the air. Chant anchored the rope by twirling the end with the grappling hook around a girder, then rolled over the railing and dropped toward the bright lights four stories below him.

Startled by Acid's panicked shriek, the three thugs dropped their handcarts and, along with the driver, glanced first at Acid dangling and struggling in the air upside down, then into the darkness over his head.

What they saw was a huge man, dressed all in black and with cold, iron-colored eyes, dropping down the rope toward them as smoke rose from the leather gloves on his hands.

The three men grabbed for their guns, but Chant had already reached the bottom, braking his descent on Acid's up-turned soles, dropping off the rope and rolling on the floor. Bullets kicked up chips of stone near his head and spine, but then he was on his feet and spinning, smashing his backpack into the face of one gunman, disabling the second man with a powerful side kick to the solar plexus, knocking the third unconscious with a forearm strike across the jaw.

Acid had managed to pull his revolver from the shoulder holster inside his jacket, but he was unable to aim properly from his upside-down position; he was firing wildly, the recoil from the large handgun making him spin and sway as he hung by his ankles from the rope. Bullets whined in the air, richocheting off the floor and steel support girders of the warehouse, smashing crates and the bottles inside. Amber-colored fluid splashed over Chant, the driver, and the three unconscious gunmen. Chant shrugged his right shoulder, and a shining, star-shaped blade fell into his palm. He flicked his wrist, and the *shuriken* whistled through the air, embedding itself in the thin man's right wrist. Acid screamed in pain, and his gun dropped from his hand to clatter on the concrete floor.

"Stay!" Chant commanded unnecessarily to the ashen-faced driver, who was crouched down between two stacks of crates, his arms over his head.

Chant walked over to Acid, who was still swaying and gripping his injured wrist as he stared at Chant, his muddy brown eyes wide with astonishment and terror. Blood flowed from his wrist and dripped off his fingertips, forming an intricate pattern of dots and splashes on the floor below his head. Without speaking, Chant reached out and casually plucked the *shuriken* from the man's wristbone, where it had stuck. As Acid shrieked again, Chant wiped the blade on the man's jacket, then put it into his pocket. He picked Acid's gun off the floor, patted the man's clothing until he felt the round, hard shape of what he was looking for, then used the stock of the revolver to smash the glass vial inside the man's pants pocket.

Acid's screaming grew in pitch and volume as the muriatic acid that had been in the vial ate through his clothes and flesh, smoking as it oozed down from his groin, across his belly, through the curve of his throat and onto his face. He died soon after the acid entered his eyes.

"Who're you?" Chant asked in Dutch as he strolled back to where the driver was still crouched on the floor.

"Holy shit," the man replied in a hoarse voice.

Chant suppressed a smile. "That's your name?"

The man gave his name, then slowly straightened up and swallowed hard. "Who are *you?*"

"You the driver of this truck?"

The man nodded nervously.

"You work for VanderKlaven?"

"No. The truck is mine. I was hired to transport this stuff to the docks and see that it was loaded. We were waiting for some guy who was supposed to show up with papers that would get the load through Customs."

"Does that sound like normal procedure to you?"

"Money isn't that easy to come by, mister. I wasn't asking questions. Look, I ain't no part of—"

"You know what's in those crates?"

The man wrinkled his nose. "It smells like medicine."

"You know where it was supposed to be shipped?"

"South Africa, I think."

"What else do you know about this shipment and what was supposed to happen here tonight? Don't try to lie to me."

"I don't know nothin' more than what I told you, mister. That's God's honest truth. I don't want to die here tonight, mister—not for the few lousy bucks I was supposed to make."

Chant studied the other man's face, decided that he was

telling the truth; he would not have profited from the sale and distribution of the adulterated antibiotics, and he had not known that a man was to be killed. "You can go," Chant said curtly. "Leave the truck here. Wait exactly one half hour, then call the local office of Interpol. Ask to speak to Inspector Bo Wahlstrom. Tell the inspector that John Sinclair sends his compliments, and there'll be something for him in the cab of your truck, which I'll park down the street. Do as you're told, and you'll get your truck back."

"You want me to call the police?"

Chant smiled thinly. "No; just Interpol. Hugo VanderKlaven's operations aren't exactly news to the Amsterdam Police."

"You John Sinclair?"

"Go! Remember: a half hour."

The man bolted away, squeezing through the narrow space between the truck bay and the warehouse doors and running off down the deserted street.

Chant waited until the echo of the driver's footsteps had died away, then turned back to examine the three gunmen. The one he had hit in the face with his backpack was just beginning to stir, and Chant clipped him on the jaw, knocking him unconscious again. From his backpack Chant removed a long, thin, glass pipette in a cushioned case. Taking the pipette in his hand, he snapped off the end, watching as a clear, viscous fluid began to ooze out of the open jagged end. Then he knelt down beside the man closest to him, turned the man's head, and slowly carved a wound just behind the man's earlobe, carefully working the thick fluid into the open cut with the broken end of the glass pipette. He repeated the procedure with the other two men, then threw the unconscious men into the back of the truck and locked the doors.

He took a packet of documents from his backpack and

carried them with him to the cab of the truck, where he taped the manila envelope beneath the dashboard. He drove the truck fifty yards down the street, parked it at the curb. He locked the doors when he got out, then threw the keys into the gutter.

Back inside the warehouse, he walked down the aisle between two stacks of crates, then knelt and set the timer on the last of the items left in his backpack—a compact but very powerful satchel charge, *plastique* with the explosive force of a dozen sticks of dynamite. This done, he walked out of the warehouse, closing the doors behind him, then disappeared silently into the Amsterdam night.

Ten minutes later a thunderous explosion shook the ground in the warehouse district, and a ball of orange fire lit up the sky as Hugo VanderKlaven's warehouse and twenty million dollars worth of medically useless antibiotics disappeared in a storm of smoke and flame.

TWO

FOR MORE THAN two decades, since walking away from the war and out of the jungles of Southeast Asia, Chant had been hunted as an international criminal; for ten years he had been the world's most wanted international criminal, and the hunt for him had been conducted with mounting frenzy and intensity. He was wanted by the police of a hundred cities, the governments of dozens of countries; he was wanted by Interpol, and he was wanted by the Americans. Especially the Americans.

There was no doubt in Chant's mind that the CIA and Interpol, separately and in cooperation, spent an enormous amount of man hours and computer time gathering information at the sites of his operations, such as the one against Hugo VanderKlaven, even as they constantly monitored international telephone traffic with the help of America's ubiquitous, enormously powerful National Security Administration with its global web of satellites and dish antennae.

Chant knew better than to underestimate the danger posed by the worldwide, electronic net that had been cast for him, and so he took security measures of his own. Years before, he had learned that the most efficient security measures were usually the simplest, and one precaution he took was never, except under the most extraordinary circumstances, to make international telephone calls to, or from, his homes. He had three principal residences—a castle in Northern Ireland, a country estate in England, and a chalet in Zermatt, Switzerland, looking out over the face of the Matterhorn. Each of the residences was listed under a different, carefully constructed identity, and staffed by personnel who owed their lives to Chant and would gladly have sacrificed themselves to protect him. Whenever Chant was away, engaged in an operation, important mail that arrived at any of his residences would be repacked and sent to him in care of a cover name at a local American Express office.

On the morning after he had blown up Hugo VanderKlaven's warehouse, Chant went to check "Rolf Bakker's" mail at the American Express office. There had been nothing for him during the time he had been in Amsterdam, but this morning there were two items inside the same packet—a small, battered package wrapped in brown manila paper, and what appeared to be a letter from Gerard Patreaux, the head of the Amnesty, Inc. office in Geneva, and Chant's friend.

Chant examined the outside of the package, noting from its various postmarks that it had originally been mailed from Lima, Peru, and that it had been in the mails for more than a month. Chant recognized the handwriting as belonging to Harry Gray, an American investigator for Amnesty,

Inc. and a friend of Chant's dating back to the war in Southeast Asia. Gray, along with Gerard Patreaux, was one of perhaps two dozen completely trusted men and women who knew all of Chant's residences, and could reach him on very short notice.

Chant tore off the wrapping paper to find a small, white cardboard box. Inside the box, nestled in a soft bed of packing material, was what appeared to be an almost perfect black pearl—the largest Chant had ever seen. Chant turned the pearl in his fingers, examining its ebony surface and mysterious, milky depths under the fluorescent light above his head, then grunted softly and put the pearl in his pocket.

There was a note—water-stained and barely legible.

A lot more where this little sucker came from. Interested? Will be back in GN in a couple of days. Call me when you're in town.
H

Chant tore up the note, threw it and the box into a wastebasket as he felt a sense of foreboding well in his heart. Then he opened the letter from Gerard Patreaux. The message inside was abrupt and to the point.

Out mutual friend HG is dead. Call me in GN if you want details.
G

Chant closed out Rolf Bakker's account with American Express, then caught a taxi to the airport where he bought a ticket for the first available flight to Geneva.

THREE

PATREAUX HAD SEEN the disguise before, and he immediately rose to his feet as the tall man with long, blond hair and dark aviator glasses walked into his office. "Hello, Chant," the slight, elegantly dressed Swiss said in French-accented English, extending his hand across the desk. "You got my message?"

"Yes," Chant replied, grasping the other man's hand as he looked into sensitive, pale blue eyes. He sat down in a leather swivel chair across the desk from the other man, removed his dark glasses, and placed them on the edge of the desk. "I was in Amsterdam. I got here as soon as I could, Gerard."

The chief administrator of Amnesty, Inc. shrugged sadly. "There wasn't any need for you to interrupt your business, my friend. There's nothing to be done. I just thought you'd want to know."

"How did Harry die, Gerard?" Chant asked quietly.

Patreaux swallowed hard and ran thin, trembling fingers through his thick, dark hair. "Very badly," he said in a barely audible whisper.

"Gerard?"

Patreaux opened a desk drawer and removed a bottle of whiskey and two glasses. He looked inquiringly at Chant, who shook his head and waited quietly as the other man poured himself a stiff drink, drank it down, and grimaced.

"His remains arrived five days ago, packed in a vacuum container," the Swiss said at last, his voice breathy and unsteady. "The package came . . . here."

"Do the police have the body in the morgue? I'd like to see it."

Patreaux shook his head. "Once the vacuum seal was broken, the remains began to decompose very rapidly. We were just barely able to perform an autopsy."

"And? What did the autopsy show?"

Patreaux again reached into his desk drawer. He removed a thin sheaf of papers that had been stapled together and handed them across the desk to Chant.

John Sinclair was truly a man of mystery, Patreaux thought as he watched the other man read the autopsy report. Many mysteries. He wondered if anyone, other than Chant himself, knew all the man's secrets—including how he had acquired his strange nickname.

At the moment, Patreaux thought, Chant was reading the almost unbelievably grisly details of the death of a man Patreaux took to be Chant's oldest and closest friend; the friend had died in a manner more horrible and terrifying than anything Patreaux had ever heard of or thought possible, and yet the other man's iron-colored eyes revealed nothing; if anything, they grew colder as they ran down the lines that described crushed bones, charred flesh, punctured organs, unnatural surgery. . . . Through it all, John

Sinclair's face remained impassive; from all outward appearances, he might have been reading a stock market report.

Yet Patreaux knew, from considerable experience, that this was one of John Sinclair's greatest strengths; he did not waste emotion. Liquor, as Patreaux well knew, could not erase the nightmare images conjured up by the words on the pages, and no amount of moaning would bring Harry Gray back to life or erase the terrible suffering he had undergone. Chant not only knew these things, Patreaux thought, but he behaved accordingly, with no futile emotion or wasted effort. Patreaux had come to consider this strange man who had become his friend as a kind of ultimate warrior; things he had been told, rumors he had heard about his friend's activities, had only served to confirm this opinion.

For some years, Patreaux had been friendly with a genial but somewhat dull-witted Baron Hoffer, a wealthy German who was a patron of the arts, a heavy financial supporter of Amnesty, Inc., and a giver of legendary parties at his huge chalet in Zermatt, looking out over the face of the Matterhorn. . . .

Harry Gray, Patreaux eventually learned, had been his "sponsor," the man who had suggested to Chant that the head of Amnesty, Inc. could be trusted with the knowledge that Baron Hoffer was in actuality not only a man who supported the organization with money, but the source, over the years, of anonymously sent packets of incredibly sensitive documents and reports that had allowed it to severely embarrass any number of governments, East and West, and organizations that sought to present one face to the world while, with their long arms flailing in dark, cold places, they broke innocent people, maimed lives.

And so Gerard Patreaux had been admitted into the

inner sanctum of the life of John Sinclair—Chant—American deserter and traitor, two-time winner of the Congressional Medal of Honor before, for reasons nobody seemed to know, he had, one day, literally walked away from the war.

And emerged an infamous legend, an international fugitive Interpol described as unbelievably dangerous and savage, a terrorizer of terrorists, but a criminal nonetheless; a victimizer of victimizers; a consummate master of disguise and accents, a linguist; the ultimate confidence man. A warrior who took no prisoners. Mercenary. Vigilante.

Patreaux knew that there were thousands of people all over the world that the "criminal" John Sinclair had helped, and who would gladly, without hesitation, sacrifice their lives for him. Patreaux, without really understanding how such intense loyalty had grown within him in such a relatively short time, was proud to consider himself a member of this group.

But the mysteries about the man persisted, and Patreaux doubted that even Harry Gray knew everything there was to know about this man Gray had once described, only half-jokingly, as a "badass Robin Hood who steals from people who steal and gives to the people who deserve it—after taking a hefty cut for himself."

Mysteries within mysteries, Patreaux thought. The persistent rumor that Interpol was under constant and relentless pressure from the CIA; the question of who had taught him his incredible martial arts skills . . . But the Swiss would never ask. What John Sinclair wanted people to know, he told them, and his friends understood this above all else.

"So," Chant said evenly, tossing the report on the desk, "Harry was tortured to death."

Patreaux swallowed hard, nodded.

"Also, somebody was snacking on him during, or between, formal sessions."

"Yes," Patreaux whispered. "The teeth marks are human. Eight of his fingers were gone, and there were chunks missing from his stomach, thighs, buttocks, and his left calf."

Chant leaned back in the chair, clasped his hands behind his head, and stared up at the ceiling. "They damn well took their time about it," he said through clenched teeth as, for the first time, his voice began to hum with emotion.

"Yes. The doctors who did the autopsy estimate between two-and-a-half and three weeks. Many of the wounds showed signs of partial healing."

"To keep him alive that long, they must have used a torture doctor."

Gerard Patreaux reached for the whiskey bottle, started to pour himself another drink, then thought better of it and pushed the bottle away. "We think so," he answered softly. "In fact, we're almost certain there was a torture doctor involved."

"What did Harry know?" Chant asked evenly, still staring at the ceiling.

"Nothing his torturers didn't know before they started on him."

Chant lowered his arms, folded his hands in his lap, and looked at the Swiss. "What did they think he knew, Gerard? What were they trying to find out?"

Again, Patreaux swallowed hard. "I don't think they were trying to find out anything."

Chant pointed to the autopsy report. "Then why . . . that? These people aren't amateurs—not when they use a torture doctor who's probably a trained surgeon."

"No," Patreaux said, his pale blue eyes suddenly glinting with rage. "We're not talking about amateurs."

Chant shook his head. "Harry wasn't trained to withstand torture. In fact, he had a low tolerance for pain—he was in trouble if he had to pull off a hangnail. Professional torturers would have known he had nothing to hide after their first pass at him. Why keep him alive for three weeks doing *that* to him?"

"Punishment," Patreaux said in a haunted voice.

"Punishment?"

"Harry knew his torturers, Chant. He'd been investigating rumors for some time, and maybe he'd finally gotten the proof we were looking for. Obviously, they caught him—and then went on to demonstrate to him just what they were capable of. So it was punishment, as well as a message to Amnesty. The body was sent to us as a demonstration that we're powerless to stop them, and as a warning to mind our own business."

"Who was Harry investigating, Gerard?"

"There's nothing you can do, Chant. For now, it seems there's nothing anybody can do."

Chant did not reply. He fixed his iron-colored eyes on Patreaux and waited.

Finally the Swiss sucked in a deep breath, let it out slowly. "There's what amounts to a torture epidemic in the world today, Chant. At our last count, at least seventy countries practice torture—or condone it by turning a blind eye and deaf ear to its use by the police or military."

"I know Amnesty has centers for victims. In fact, you have one here in Geneva."

Patreaux nodded. "We get thousands of victims, and yet surprisingly little is known about how to treat them. You're right; we operate a number of centers around the world for victims of torture. It's a practice, an abomination, Amnesty, Inc. takes very seriously. Harry took it personally; for the past two years he focused on nothing but torture investigations."

"I know," Chant said quietly. He was impatient to learn the identities of Harry's torturers, but sensed that Gerard Patreaux was attempting to exorcise his own nightmares and needed to give the information in his own way, in his own time.

"Amnesty's been engaged in a two-pronged attack," Patreaux said, lighting a cigarette. "First, we try to expose the practice of official, governmental torture and hope that world opinion will have some effect. Second, as I said, we try to help the survivors. One of the most astounding things our psychiatrists have to deal with is the strong emotional bond—it would be too perverse to describe it as a kind of love, but it can resemble that—that sometimes develops between the victim and his or her torturer. That bond can be very difficult to break, and we just don't understand enough about all the complex mental processes at work. Almost all victims endure years of depression; they can only sleep two or three hours a night, and they spend the rest of the time pacing. Large numbers commit suicide. Many become impotent, and it's not uncommon for them to suffer intense pains that have no physical cause. Incredibly, many suffer crushing guilt—they blame themselves, especially if other members of their families have been tortured because of their activities. They become suspicious to the point of paranoia. Torture is so individually focused that it destroys the mechanics by which we deal with people and solve everyday problems. It turns the brain to soup." Patreaux paused, glanced up at Chant. "But you don't care about any of this—you want to know who went to work on Harry."

"I am interested, Gerard—and I do want to know who tortured and killed Harry. But I'm in no hurry. I want to know anything you care to tell me."

Patreaux, whose voice and manner had become steadier as he'd spoken, nodded curtly, rose, and walked around his desk to where a rack of maps on spring rollers was mounted on the wall. Patreaux pulled one of the maps down, and Chant found himself looking at the western half of South America.

"Actually," Patreaux said in a low voice, without turning, "Harry wasn't even supposed to be where I suspect he ended up. He'd originally gone to Nicaragua to negotiate with the Sandinistas for permission to interview and study some of the torturers from the Somoza regime they've got locked up down there."

"What would be the point, Gerard?"

The Swiss shrugged. "There are psychiatrists who believe that studying the mind of the torturer may help us to better understand the mind of the victim—for example, the emotional bond I mentioned. Also, it could give governments that want to *avoid* torture some idea of the personality types that require close supervision, if they're to do police or military work at all."

"Obviously," Chant said in a flat voice, "the torturers Harry found weren't locked up."

"Probably here," Patreaux said, putting the tip of his index finger beneath a tiny dot in the Pacific, just off the coast of Chile.

"What's there?"

"It's all supposition, Chant. Rumor."

"It's rumor Harry acted on, maybe after he got a tip in Nicaragua. What do you think is on that island, Gerard?"

Now Patreaux turned. His face was slightly ashen, and his mouth was set in a firm line. "The name of the island in Spanish means 'Place of Winds.' We call it Torture Island. If our information is correct, there's a kind of torture institute out there."

"A torture *institute?*"

The Swiss nodded. "Yes—by which I mean a facility devoted to the refining and improvement of techniques and tools for torture. Just what the world needs. There are governments, and even some private organizations, who'll pay a lot of money for that kind of information and training. It's run by a prince of a man named Dr. Richard Krowl; he's an American who was thrown out of medical school for conducting unauthorized experiments."

"What kind of experiments?"

"We've never been able to find out; the record is sealed, and the school won't talk. However, I think it's safe to assume that the experiments would have done someone like Josef Mengele proud. Anyway, Krowl must have seen that there was money to be made in the torture business—and he's making it. Some of the worst torturers in the world show up on that island for Krowl's seminars and demonstrations. He runs a pretty sophisticated operation in pain and death."

"I wouldn't think governments that torture would suffer any shortage of would-be torturers," Chant said. "And almost any physician with a streak of the sadist in him will make a fairly decent torture doctor. Why pay Krowl? What's so special about him?"

Patreaux shrugged sadly. "That's what I assume Harry was trying to pin down. We just don't know that much about him or his operation. However, I suppose he's just the best there is at what he does. He handles very special cases. If all you want to do is intimidate, brutalize, terrorize, or punish, then any idiot with pincers and a cattle prod can do the job—assuming you're not worried about the victim dying, or what he looks like when the idiot is finished with him. As we both know, that isn't always the case. If the authorities want to extract information from a very tough man—somebody like you, for example—there could be a problem. You'd evade and defy. They wouldn't care what you ended up looking like, but they wouldn't want you to die before you told them what they wanted to know—and they'd want to make certain the information was accurate. That would take some doing. Then you have political prisoners, people like Viktor and Olga Petroff who have gained the attention of the world. The Russians would probably do anything to get Viktor Petroff to shut up or recant, but they can't afford to mark up him or his wife because too many people are watching. Tough, resistant people like you, or people like the Petroffs who require kid-glove treatment, give torturers fits. Also, there's only so much pain a person can endure before passing out, or dying."

"Which is why we have torture doctors," Chant said in the same, flat voice.

"Right. A good torture doctor can maximize pain in a victim, while assuring that the person doesn't die before his torturers want him to—which is exactly what was done with Harry. If our information is correct, Krowl gets special cases from a lot of different countries. He conducts the torture sessions while torturers whose governments have paid for them to be there watch and listen. At least, that's what we suspect goes on. He doesn't exactly publish a newsletter. The island is isolated, and his operation there is protected by the countries whose interests he serves."

"What countries?"

"A very good question, and one we'd dearly love to know the answer to. Some, like the seventy I mentioned, would be obvious customers, but we think Krowl may have some other customers who aren't so obvious—both East and West bloc. That's what Harry was working on. If we could get hard evidence that major powers, communist or democratic, have ever sent—or do send—prisoners to Krowl, the publicity would be devastating. The uproar would probably be enough to shut down Torture Island."

"When you say 'countries,' I assume you're talking about intelligence or internal security agencies."

"In most cases, yes. In eastern bloc countries, the distinctions become blurred."

"Do the Russians use Krowl?"

Patreaux shrugged. "Maybe. We don't know."

"The CIA?"

"Same answer, Chant. I do know that the possibility bothered Harry a lot."

Chant grunted softly, then pointed to the map. "Are there black pearls in that area of the Pacific?"

"As a matter of fact, there are," the Swiss said, obviously puzzled by the change of subject and the question. "How do you—?"

Patreaux stopped speaking when Chant took something out of his pocket and rolled it across the desk. Patreaux just managed to catch it before it rolled off the edge of the desk, and he stared in astonishment at the huge black pearl in his hand.

"Harry sent that to me," Chant said evenly. "Judging from the postmark on the package, he must have dropped it in the mail just before he was captured."

Patreaux frowned. "There are stories—legends, really—about there being rich beds of oysters that produce black pearls in that region of the ocean; there are also stories about Krowl having amassed a fortune in them. If he has, I don't know how he did it. The waters around that island are among the most shark-infested in the world; there are hammerheads, makos, blues—just about every species you can name, including an occasional great white. That's why nobody dives for the black pearls that are supposed to be there. Where could Harry have gotten this?"

"He mailed the package from Lima, and I doubt that he found it on the sidewalk there."

"Why did he send it to you?" Patreaux asked, still obviously distracted by the pearl in his hand.

"He must have thought I'd be interested in the good Dr. Krowl and his doings."

Patreaux set the pearl back down on the desk and shook his head. "It's not your kind of operation, Chant. You always work alone, and you know that deception, disguise, concealment, and surprise are important. That won't work on Torture Island. It's too small, and Krowl's facility is the only thing there—if it *is* there. Krowl would know everybody there."

Chant pointed to the pearl. "Harry must have gotten on the island, and off again. He made it to Peru."

Patreaux, still unconvinced, shook his head. "I don't understand how Harry could have done it. The island is twenty miles off the coast—too far to swim, even if there weren't the sharks. And the island is surrounded by coral reefs. It's only accessible by air."

"Then where did Harry get the pearl?"

"I don't know, Chant," Patreaux said softly. "I do know that I've lost a dear and courageous friend, and I don't want to lose another. Harry's death has provided me with enough horror to last a lifetime. God, Chant, I wish you *could* give Krowl and his torturers a bit of special attention, but everything I've ever heard about the island indicates that there's no way. Putting Krowl out of business is a job for civilized nations. There's nothing one individual—not even John Sinclair—can do. As I said, you couldn't even get on the island."

Chant reached out for the pearl, casually dropped it in his shirt pocket. He lifted the bottle, poured drinks for both of them. "Here's to Harry," Chant said, raising his glass.

"To Harry," Gerard Patreaux responded, his pale blue eyes misting as he raised his own glass and drank with Chant.

"What's the latest on Viktor and Olga Petroff?" Chant

asked quietly as he set his glass down beside the bottle.

The eyes of the Amnesty, Inc. chief glinted with anger. "Nobody's heard anything for two weeks, not since the Russians packed them off to Gorky. The official line is that they're still in Gorky, alive and well and probably rethinking all the nasty things they've said about the Soviet system."

"A newspaper in Holland reported they'd both gone on a hunger strike and were being force-fed."

"We've heard that rumor, but there's no solid evidence to show they're even still in Gorky. We have some contacts in Gorky, but they don't report seeing any sign of the Petroffs. There've been no smuggled letters, nothing."

"Would the Russians dare put them in a mental institution?"

"They might; they're getting pretty desperate. They claim they can't allow the Petroffs out of the country because both are nuclear scientists and privy to too many defense secrets. On the other hand, every time the authorities turn their backs the Petroffs call a press conference and denounce the abuse of human rights. At least they did before the Soviets packed them off to Gorky. It's a closed city."

"Yes," Chant answered absently. He was again leaning back in his chair, staring up at the ceiling.

"You said you were in Amsterdam?"

"Yes."

"On business, I presume?"

Chant nodded.

"If you don't mind, I'd love to hear about it. It always makes me feel better when I learn that John Sinclair has mounted an operation against some poor, misunderstood soul."

Chant looked at his friend, smiled wryly. "The poor, misunderstood soul in Amsterdam is a pharmaceuticals mogul named Hugo VanderKlaven. His operation is a bit complicated, but what it boils down to is the sale of adulterated antibiotics to Third World and underdeveloped countries. He has a whole string of corrupt officials he's bribed. The officials arrange for public health administrators in their various governments to buy their drugs from VanderKlaven. What they get is medicine that's been cut three or four times. In more advanced countries, he sells his shit on the black market."

"But antibiotics that have been cut like that would be worthless."

"Precisely. Patients injected with VanderKlaven's drugs don't respond, and they usually die. Their doctors might as well have injected them with water."

"I'm surprised the doctors haven't suspected the drugs are bad."

Chant shrugged. "The doctors who receive the drugs don't operate practices in New York or London. They're harried, overworked public health physicians fighting what's already a tidal wave of death in places like South Africa's black relocation areas, or the poorest areas of India. So many people die on them anyway, the doctors don't suspect that the antibiotics they've been using might be bad. Besides, they have no testing facilities."

"Jesus!" Patreaux said with disgust. "I've been doing work like the work I do for Amnesty for more than twenty years, and I still find it hard to believe the cruelty some humans will inflict on other humans—sometimes for revenge, sometimes out of anger, and other times just to make money."

"Shall I bring Hugo VanderKlaven to you, Gerard?" Chant asked with only the slightest trace of irony in his voice. "You can interview him and ask him why he wants to do such nasty things."

Patreaux laughed easily. "Ah, I see you don't think

much of the idea of studying torturers to see what makes them tick."

"It would be presumptuous of me to offer an opinion one way or the other; I'm not a psychiatrist. I believe, simply, that some men and women are evil, and that's all there is to it. Torturers are in their line of work because it gives them pleasure to see people suffer and die. People like VanderKlaven do what they do because they have sociopathic personalities, and making money is all that matters to them."

Chant paused, poured another drink for himself and Patreaux. "Men like VanderKlaven have very little imagination when it comes to the suffering of others," he continued evenly, sipping the malt Scotch. "It might be interesting to see how he would respond to having an illness his frustrated doctors couldn't treat. The same for the men who work for him. For example, there's a microscopic parasite that lives in the mud of the Amazon Basin. Some natives pick it up when they bathe or wash clothes in the river. The parasite can only enter the body through breaks in the skin, but when it does get in the bloodstream it wreaks havoc in a relatively short period of time—often three weeks or less. It multiplies rapidly in human blood, and it goes straight for the organs of the head. It loves to feast on the brain, and it gets there by chewing its way along the optic nerve."

"Oh, my God," Patreaux murmured with a shudder of revulsion.

"Before the victim dies, he or she goes blind and suffers considerable agony. There's no drug powerful enough to kill the parasite without killing the patient, so it can be said there's no cure. It would be interesting to see how somebody like VanderKlaven and the others who knowingly profit from what he does would like being inoculated with a culture containing a strain of that parasite. After all, it would make their situation somewhat analogous to the men, women, and children with things like diphtheria or cholera who didn't respond to the watered-down medicine administered to them."

"Oh, Jesus," Patreaux said in a cracked voice as he realized that this was precisely what Chant had done—or would do. As had happened so many times in the past, the Swiss found himself at once horrified and thrilled by the acts Chant was capable of. John Sinclair, he thought, might strike terror in the hearts of countless people, but it could never be said that he wasn't extremely selective when it came to choosing his victims.

Chant rose, extended his hand across the desk. "Now I have to go back to finish up my business with VanderKlaven, Gerard. You know how much I appreciate your letting me know about Harry."

Patreaux rose, gripped Chant's hand firmly with both of his. "Thanks for coming, my friend; it's made me feel better just talking to you. I hope we'll see each other soon—under better circumstances."

"Yes," Chant replied evenly, staring hard into the other man's face. "In the meantime, there's something I'd like you to do for me."

"Chant, you know I'd do anything you ask—assuming it's in my power."

"I'm glad you feel that way, Gerard," Chant said with just the faintest trace of a smile, "because you're not going to like this at all."

FOUR

CHANT SPENT THE first day at his country estate in England planning and writing a series of coded cables to be sent out by his aides at prearranged dates.

On the second day, with the expert help of a young Japanese woman who was his pupil as well as his assistant, he prepared his body.

The third day was spent alone meditating, hiking his fields, gazing into the depths of his ponds and lakes, preparing his mind. His only companion was fear, with which he carried on a silent, internal dialogue. Confronting his fear, imagining the worst things that could happen to him, he was able to conquer it, at least for the time being, and prevent it from distracting him; for he knew that once he began he would have to proceed step-by-step with no fear and no hesitation. Once he had begun this journey, there could be no turning back.

For the first time in his life Chant engaged in the intricate meditative procedure that would, if there was truth in the legends, arm him with a most potent secret weapon. Chant had been told that less than one hundred men had been taught the secret since the seventh century, and he was the only Occidental. This secret was the greatest gift, the highest honor, Chant had ever received, and it afforded him the one weapon that assured that he could, finally, never be totally defeated, except by himself.

On the morning of the fourth day he left for Amsterdam.

FIVE

AT PRECISELY TWO o'clock in the afternoon, Chant walked into the lobby of the three-story building housing VanderKlaven Pharmaceuticals. He smiled thinly when he felt the air of almost palpable tension emanating from a few of the staff members he passed on the way to the elevators; it meant the police were starting to make some moves—slow moves, perhaps, but moves nonetheless. Although Interpol had no jurisdiction over Amsterdam proper, Inspector Bo Wahlstrom was making his presence felt. Pressure was being applied.

Chant waited until he was alone, then entered an elevator and pressed the Basement button; there were three more of the Dutchman's employees he wished to visit, the enforcers in VanderKlaven's satellite operations in narcotics and child prostitution.

The elevator stopped, the doors sighed open onto a narrow, dank stone corridor. Chant turned to his left and walked quickly toward the small office where he knew VanderKlaven's "maintenance men" sat, drank, and played cards while they waited for any orders that might be forthcoming from their boss. The door at the end of the corridor was open, and Chant stepped into the doorway, filling it, fixing his gaze on the three men who sat around a small table in the center of the room, studying the grimy cards they had just been dealt.

"Hey, what the hell?!" one of the men shouted as he glanced up and saw Chant. He sprang to his feet, knocking over his chair, drew a gun, and started to walk forward. "What are you doing here? Who are you?"

"I seem to be lost," Chant said, affecting surprise at the sight of the gun in the hand of the man who was approaching him.

"Well, mister, you get your ass back to the elevator and up—"

Chant's left hand darted out and snatched the gun from the other man's hand. At the same time, Chant's right elbow flew into the man's throat with a force that instantly crushed the larynx and snapped his neck. Chant put a single bullet into the foreheads of the other two gunmen even as they were struggling to get their own guns out of their holsters. Then Chant threw the gun into the room among the corpses, turned, and headed back toward the elevator.

He would have liked to inoculate the three gunmen with the parasite instead of killing them outright, but he had only one pipette of the culture left.

"Bakker!" Hugo VanderKlaven shouted, jumping up from behind his desk as Chant entered the office, closing the door behind him. The obese man ran a bejeweled index finger across his upper lip, wiping away sweat. "Why didn't my secretary announce you?"

"She seems to have stepped out for a few minutes," Chant replied easily, walking across the office and sitting down in a chair on the other side of the Dutchman's desk. "What's the matter, VanderKlaven? You look surprised to see me."

VanderKlaven again nervously swiped his finger across his upper lip, then slowly eased his massive body down into the chair behind his desk. Behind the thick lenses of his glasses, his small, black eyes burned even brighter than usual. His suit jacket was draped over the back of his chair, and his baby-blue silk shirt was darkening with blotches of sweat. "What do you want, Bakker?"

"What do I want? I believe you owe me money—a million pounds sterling, to be exact."

"You double-crossed me!" VanderKlaven shouted, pounding a fat fist on his desk, sending papers flying. "I never trusted you, Bakker, and I was right! You were supposed to meet me at my warehouse five nights ago to deliver the government authorizations and Customs documents! Where the hell were you?!"

"Oh, I was there," Chant said evenly, smiling thinly as he saw VanderKlaven reach beneath his desk to push the button that would activate an alarm down in the office of his "maintenance men." "There seemed to be a bit of a commotion, so I decided it might be better to wait and come here to see you. I also thought it might be safer. I knew you didn't much care for me, and it occurred to me that you just might be planning to kill me and save yourself a payment. After all, you could always find somebody else in South Africa to do business with."

"Somebody blew up my warehouse, Bakker!" VanderKlaven shouted, glancing up nervously at the door behind Chant. "And copies of those phony inspection documents ended up in the hands of the police!"

"Really? Too bad. Incidentally, if you're waiting for

your men to show up, you're going to be disappointed. They've stepped out too."

VanderKlaven started, glanced sharply at Chant. Now fear moved in his eyes. "Who are you, Bakker? Interpol? Police?"

"Not likely. I'm a man you owe money to."

"You're insane. I don't even have the goods anymore."

Chant shrugged. "I don't see how that concerns me, VanderKlaven. That's your problem. I want my money, and I know you have enough to cover it in that safe behind you."

The fat Dutchman flushed, half rose out of his chair. "You'll get nothing from me, Bakker! Why should I give you money?!"

"Because I'll kill you if you don't."

VanderKlaven grabbed for the telephone on his desk. Chant rose and swept the phone off the desk with an easy swipe of his hand. Then he clipped the Dutchman once, hard, on the collarbone with the edge of his palm. The fat man's right arm went limp. VanderKlaven fell out of his chair onto the floor, clutching his broken shoulder, moaning and writhing in agony.

"Shut up," Chant said, coming around the desk and standing over VanderKlaven. "If you don't do as I say, I'll break your other collarbone and you'll have to open the safe with your toes."

Spittle ran out of the other man's white lips as he groaned and shook his head. "There's no money in the safe."

"Wrong. The last time I looked in there, there was—besides your records—my million pounds, fifteen million Dutch florins, and five million Swiss francs." He paused, smiled thinly as the other man gaped at him in astonishment. "How else could I have copied all your records if I didn't break into your safe?" he continued easily. "I'd open it again myself, but I didn't bring my equipment with me."

VanderKlaven gasped in astonishment as Chant casually removed his black wig, ducked his head and removed his green-tinted contact lenses. *"Who are you?!"*

Chant picked up VanderKlaven's large leather briefcase from beside the desk, emptied out the contents, and tossed it next to the man. "Put the money in there, VanderKlaven. You're starting to piss me off, so now I'll have you put it all in. Do it!"

"You're a dead man," VanderKlaven murmured between clenched teeth as he got up on his hands and knees and began to work the dial of the large safe. "You'll never get away with this. You're a . . . a *thief!*"

"I love it, VanderKlaven," Chant said as he watched the other man shovel the cash inside the safe into the briefcase. He glanced at his watch, saw that it was 2:35. He took the full briefcase from VanderKlaven, then motioned for the other man to sit back down in his chair.

"My arm's broken," the Dutchman whined. "I need medical attention."

"You'll need an undertaker if you don't sit your fat ass down in that chair."

VanderKlaven struggled to his feet and, still gripping his broken shoulder, slumped in his chair. Chant walked back around the desk, sat down on the edge.

"What are you going to do?" VanderKlaven asked in a trembling voice. "You've got my money. What else do you want?"

Chant raised his eyebrows slightly. "I want to chat."

"What?"

"I want to ask you a question."

VanderKlaven's lids narrowed. "What kind of a question?"

"Why do you do what you do?"

VanderKlaven shook his head. "I don't understand."

"You own one of the biggest pharmaceuticals manufacturing and distribution concerns in the world. *Legitimately,* you earn millions of dollars a year off the drugs you manufacture and the patents you own. Why, then, peddle useless drugs that doom people to die of diseases they'd otherwise be cured of? Why peddle heroin and cocaine? Why prostitute children, for Christ's sake?"

Again, VanderKlaven shook his head—this time in bewilderment. "To make *more* money, of course."

Chant grunted. "That's what I thought."

"What kind of a stupid question is that?"

"Just a question."

"Why should a thief ask a question like that?"

"Motives are a subject that interest a friend of mine," Chant replied easily, once again glancing at his watch. It was 2:45.

Chant abruptly leaned over the desk and brought the side of his hand up under VanderKlaven's jaw, knocking him unconscious and back out of his chair. He took his last glass pipette from his pocket, broke off the end, moved around the desk and ground the glass and parasite culture into the flesh behind VanderKlaven's left ear. Then he picked up the bulging briefcase and walked unhurriedly from the office.

When he had come in, at least two dozen people had been busy in other offices or scurrying up and down the wide, carpeted hallway. Now the entire floor was deserted, which did not surprise Chant. Everyone had been evacuated—quickly, efficiently, silently.

At the end of the corridor, in the vestibule before the elevators, Chant found a man waiting for him. Clad only in undershorts, the man was seated on the floor, legs crossed Indian fashion, hands visible and empty, back braced against the wall between two elevators. The man appeared to be in his late fifties or early sixties, but was in exceptional physical condition. Chant estimated him to be just under six feet, around a hundred and eighty pounds. There were the telltale pockmark scars of bullet wounds in his left shoulder and right thigh. He had a full head of light brown hair only now turning to gray, deep brown eyes that gleamed with intelligence and toughness that was tempered with compassion. The eyes were fixed intently on Chant as he approached, stopped, and stood over the man.

"Good afternoon, Inspector Wahlstrom," Chant said easily, a faint smile tugging at the corners of his mouth. "I see you're unarmed. You have an interesting way of making a point."

"You know who I am." It was not a question. The man's voice was a deep, melodious rumble originating deep in his chest. The tone reflected resolve, wariness but not fear.

"I've seen your picture."

Wahlstrom's laugh displayed nervousness. "Oh, I've seen yours too. The problem is that all the photographs of you are at least twenty years old. Descriptions of you are worthless; I've never heard two people describe you in the same way. The only thing they all agree on is that you're a crazy son of a bitch who scared the shit out of them."

"I'll have to hire a new public relations firm."

"Is this what you really look like?"

"This is it, Inspector."

Wahlstrom nodded down the corridor behind Chant. "Did you leave that monster alive?"

"Mr. VanderKlaven? He's just unconscious—but he doesn't look too well. I think the man may be ill."

"Could he have caught the same bug as the three men you left for me in the back of that truck outside the warehouse?"

Chant shrugged. "I believe that's very possible," he said with a thin smile.

"Those three are being kept in isolation in the hospital.

The doctors can't seem to be able to figure out what's wrong with them."

"Isolation seems like a good idea. However, I suspect there's no danger to hospital personnel as long as they observe normal procedures and don't get any blood or fecal matter in open cuts."

"I'll pass your thoughts on to the appropriate hospital personnel. Any idea what's wrong with them?"

"I wouldn't presume to guess," Chant said, setting the briefcase down, then sitting on the floor and leaning against the wall across the corridor from the Interpol inspector.

"You do good work, Sinclair," he said. "There are one hell of a lot of very nasty people around the world who haven't had a decent night's sleep in fifteen years, worrying that John Sinclair is going to pay them a visit and do some kind of number on them. I thank you for the information you sent me on VanderKlaven, as well as all the other tips and documents you've fed to me over the years. The information has been put to good use."

"I know that. You do good work, too, Inspector. It's why you received the tips." He paused, smiled. "After all, I'm a busy man—or I was. I couldn't handle all the business, so I always figured I could send a few deserving people your way."

"I've been promoted many times because of arrests I've made based on information you've fed me."

"Good. You've deserved them."

"It can't make a difference in this situation, Sinclair."

"If I'd ever thought you wouldn't do your job because of personal feelings, I wouldn't have fed you information. However, judging from your appearance in the building, I'd say it's already made a difference. You couldn't be certain I wouldn't throw you down an elevator shaft."

"Somehow, I didn't think you would."

"How did you know I'd be here?"

Wahlstrom shrugged and grimaced, as if embarrassed. "An anonymous tip. The man who called knew enough about you to make us take him seriously. Frankly, I'm surprised you came back. After giving me the documents and all of VanderKlaven's records, you must have known the police would be forced to start tightening a net around him. Even if I hadn't been tipped off that you'd be here, it was still risky for you to walk into this building."

"I'm used to working in tight quarters. Maybe I just got overconfident."

Wahlstrom narrowed his lids, studied Chant for some time before saying, "I don't believe that. Do you have any idea who it was that called me?"

"No."

"How many people could have known where you'd be today, and at what time?"

"I must have left my appointment book lying around. You sound downright disappointed that you've nabbed me, Inspector. Would you like me to leave and come back on another day when you're in a better mood?"

Wahlstrom stiffened and flushed slightly with anger. "Will you surrender and come downstairs with me?"

"What are my options, Inspector?"

"There is only one, Sinclair: You can die. I'm well aware of your reputation for being able to vanish into thin air, but we both know that's not really possible. You can't escape. There are a hundred policemen surrounding this building, and snipers on the rooftops with orders to shoot to kill if you do try to escape. Frankly, the Americans are most anxious that you not be killed; they want Interpol to take you in custody and hold you incommunicado until they can take possession of you. But Interpol does not work for the Americans, and we will do what is necessary to stop you—including gunning you down, if it comes to that. That's what I came up here to tell you. My men will shoot if you don't surrender."

"What if I'm using you as a shield?"

"They'll still shoot."

"It took considerable courage for you to come up here. In fact, I suspect it may be a highly unofficial visit. Do your superiors know you're here?"

"They do by now."

"Ah, you could be in some trouble, Inspector. You're risking your career as well as your life. Why?"

"I told you; I feel I owe you."

"Why? Because I provided you with a few tips? I told you I have more business than I can handle."

"I feel I owe you because you are a just, honest, decent man. I don't want you to die."

Chant laughed. "I'm a criminal, Inspector."

"Yes, you are that too," Wahlstrom replied simply. "Which is why we find ourselves in this unfortunate situation. I wish I were a big enough man to have ignored the information about your being in this building, but it was not possible. I can sacrifice my pension, and even my life, but I cannot fail to do my job; work, finally, is what gives a man dignity. I'm sorry it has to be this way."

"I always understood that we were on opposite sides of the law, Inspector."

"We do need law."

"I couldn't agree more."

"Don't die in Amsterdam, John Sinclair."

"All right," Chant said easily, rising to his feet and extending his hand to help the other man up. "Let's go, Inspector. I don't want you to catch cold, and I certainly don't want you to lose your pension."

SIX

CHANT, NAKED, SAT on the floor of the bare, windowless cell, relaxing and once again focusing his mind on the procedures he would have to use to trigger his final, most powerful weapon. In effect, he was practicing something that could not be practiced, trying to prepare himself for a feat that could probably only be accomplished once—if at all.

Somewhere down the long corridor outside his cell a door clanged open and footsteps approached. Chant turned his head, found Bo Wahlstrom standing outside his cell. The Inspector's face was flushed, and his lips were pressed tightly together.

"I am sorry for the indignities you must suffer, Sinclair," he said in a strained voice. "I argued strongly against these precautions, but I did not prevail."

"What indignities?" Chant said easily, rising and walking across the cell to stand at the bars. Wahlstrom did not shy away, as Chant had suspected he might. In the twenty-four hours that had passed since he had been thrown naked into the naked cell, he suspected that the Interpol inspector had heard a lot of strange stories about him from a lot of different, strange people. "Frankly, I'm surprised to see you. Yours wasn't the first face I expected to see."

"As I've told you, Interpol is not an agency of the United States government."

"That's true, but I thought we were trying to save your pension."

"If I lose my pension, it won't be the CIA that takes it away. We caught you. As I see it, that gives us the right to interrogate you first—and the Americans can yell all they want."

"Is this an interrogation?"

"Are you warm enough?"

"Yes. As a matter of fact, it's a bit too warm. You can turn the temperature down a few degrees, if you'd care to."

"I'll take care of it. The fact that you can have nothing in your cell, not even clothes to wear, is ridiculous—but it's a concession we felt we had to make to the CIA for not turning you over to them right away. I'm sorry."

"It's not important, Inspector."

"To me, it is. I consider being forced to sit naked in an absolutely bare cell, to even be forced to eat food with your fingers off paper plates, terrible indignities."

"I've told you I feel no indignity," Chant replied evenly. "Incidentally, the food is very good."

"I oversee its preparation myself. It's the least I can do, considering the fact that you surrendered yourself into my custody and now you must suffer . . . *this*."

"Thank you."

"I'll at least bring you a pillow," he said forcefully. "They can't object to that."

"Don't bring me anything, Inspector. Believe me, they'll object."

"What on earth do they think you could do with a *pillow?*"

"You'll have to ask them."

Wahlstrom inclined his head, fixed his deep, brown eyes on Chant, and studied him for a few moments. "With precautions like these, it would appear that the CIA was concerned about you committing suicide. But that's not what it's about, is it?"

"Something else you'll have to ask them, Inspector."

"Mmm. I think not. They really do seem to believe that you can find a way to use virtually anything as a weapon, or as a means of escape." The Interpol inspector paused, narrowed his lids as he studied the man who was standing less than an arm's length away, leaning casually on the bars. "Can you really do all the things they say you can do?"

Chant shrugged. "I don't know what they say I can do."

"Your countrymen are very much afraid of you, John Sinclair."

"Not all my countrymen, Inspector. Not even the CIA proper. A few men in the agency and at various levels of government are afraid of me, and they have good reason to be."

"Why?"

Chant said nothing.

"At first I thought it was something you knew that they wanted to know, but that didn't seem to make sense. What secrets could you possess that would still be so valuable to them after all these many years?"

"Ah, the interrogation," Chant said with a thin smile. "Not a good idea. It probably isn't even a good idea for you to spend so much time alone with me, Inspector. As you've suspected for years, and now know for sure, my biggest enemies are very nervous and jealous men. They won't like the fact that you're talking to me."

"The Americans' obsession with you fascinates me, Sinclair. It's a mystery."

"Perhaps it's better if it stays that way."

"For my benefit?"

"For everyone's benefit."

"Then it *is* something you know!"

"Is it, Inspector?"

"You won't answer any of my questions, will you?"

"It seems to me that I've already answered a few."

"But you won't tell me why the CIA has been so desperate for twenty years to get hold of you?"

"No. I won't tell you that."

"They say you're a traitor."

"Do they?"

"I know that you deserted from the army during your country's war in Southeast Asia. That much is in your file. You were a captain in the Special Forces—the youngest captain, I believe. Incredibly, that's all there is in your file regarding your service record. Obviously, you must have been a CIA operative at the same time as you were serving in the army."

"Mmmm."

"The Americans are hiding a lot, aren't they?"

"Are they?"

"Also, I suspect a great deal of truth about you and your service to your country has been distorted by them. Did you really desert?"

"Yes," Chant answered simply.

Something dark moved in the Interpol inspector's brown eyes. "I find it difficult to believe that you're a traitor."

"'Desertion' is the description of an act. What I did fits

that description. 'Traitor' is a term that's somewhat more judgmental, so I leave it for others to concern themselves with. It's not something I give a lot of thought to."

Wahlstrom frowned, shook his head slightly. "Why did you desert, Sinclair?"

Chant did not reply.

"Is the reason you deserted the same reason the Americans have been so desperate to get hold of you? Is it related?"

Still Chant did not reply.

"Was it a matter of conscience?"

"It was a matter of death."

"Your death?"

"Death."

"Will you give me a statement concerning your activities over the past twenty years?"

Chant laughed. "There isn't much that I've done that isn't in Interpol's files."

"Those are other people's statements. Will you give me yours?"

"No."

"You don't seem all that upset about being captured."

"Would it do me any good to be upset?"

"No. Will you tell me how we might be able to recover any of the money you've stolen?"

"No. If I told you that, it would only go back to the crooks I stole it from in the first place. *That* would upset me."

Wahlstrom chuckled. "Where have you been living all these years, Sinclair?"

"I won't tell you that either, Inspector."

Wahlstrom sighed, studied Chant. "The CIA wants you very badly."

"So you've indicated."

"What will they do with you?"

"I haven't got the slightest idea. I'm sure they won't feed me as well as the Dutch have."

"They can't just take you away, you know. There are international laws to be observed, and you're not in their custody yet. The U.S. Army has waived its jurisdiction, as have the U.S. courts. The European nations will certainly waive theirs to please the Americans. The Communists, as usual, will ignore you. To do otherwise would be to admit that you've made them look as foolish as everyone else you've ever gone against. Still, I suggest that you can resist in the courts here. You might be able to resist extradition. Perhaps there are other avenues to explore."

"Are you going to act as my lawyer, Inspector?"

"You're mocking me."

"On the contrary; I'm thanking you."

"You could appeal to the Dutch courts to take jurisdiction."

"It won't work, Inspector. But thanks for the thought."

Wahlstrom stared hard at Chant for some time, his eyes troubled, then abruptly turned and started to walk away. He slowed, came to a stop, turned back.

"What is it, Inspector?" Chant asked quietly.

"John Sinclair, I'm sorry."

"About what?"

"This is the first time we've met face-to-face, yet in all the years that I've been chasing you I've come to respect—and, yes, admire—you a great deal. Yes, you are a criminal—a thief, a murderer who often kills his victims in a brutal fashion. The difference between you and others is that the people you prey on have themselves chosen to operate outside the law, and *their* victims are innocent. You've saved the lives of countless people, helped countless others. You've helped me. That I should be responsible for—this—just doesn't seem right."

"Your guilt is misplaced, Inspector. You had to do your

job, and you did it. You feel guilty because we hate the same kinds of people, the same things. You are a just man who's outraged by corruption and cruelty—"

"So are you, John Sinclair."

"No. You're an officer of the law who hunts these people out of honor and a search for justice; I'm a businessman who hunts them for money."

Wahlstrom shook his head. "No," he said simply. "There is much more to you than that."

"You fail to appreciate the fact that criminals make relatively easy victims; they have too much to hide, and they are very vulnerable to somebody using the right techniques. Since they've chosen to perform acts that are illegal, they can't very well go to the law for help when I attack them. It's just good business."

"God, you wreak such terrible vengeance," Wahlstrom said softly. "But I don't believe that you've done it for money—despite the fortune I know you've amassed. In fact, John Sinclair, I believe you are the most just and honorable man I have ever met. And that is why I feel guilty."

Chant shrugged, smiled. "Inspector, you're starting to make *me* feel bad. I've lived very well for years doing the things I did. Now that I've been caught, I have no regrets. I always knew I wasn't a good candidate for retirement."

"Tell me why the Americans want you, Sinclair. I may be able to help."

"There are only a few Americans who want me for reasons other than the ones you've wanted me for, Inspector. There's nothing you can do. If I were to share that information with you, I'd be signing your death warrant."

"They can't be that powerful."

Chant's smile vanished, and his iron-gray eyes grew cold and dangerous. "We'll see how powerful they are, Inspector. And that's all I'll have to say on the matter."

"Will they hurt you?"

"Good-bye, Inspector. It's been a pleasure dealing with you over the years."

Wahlstrom extended his hand, and Chant gripped it firmly. Then the Interpol inspector turned and walked away. This time the footsteps did not stop. However, the great door at the end of the corridor did not clang shut.

A second set of footsteps—slow and purposeful, somehow ominous—approached.

"Back off, Sinclair," the man with the cold eyes and American-accented English said, "or you'll get this gas grenade in the belly."

Chant did as he was told, and the man in the light brown suit pulled the trigger on his air gun. The gas grenade skipped off the stone floor a few feet away from Chant and exploded against the wall. Chant quickly sat down so that he would not injure himself by falling. As he breathed in the pink smog filling the cell and felt his limbs go numb, it occurred to him that Bo Wahlstrom's was the last friendly face he was likely to see for a long time; indeed, it could have been the last friendly face he would ever see.

SEVEN

HE WAS COLD, although he sensed that someone had dressed him. Occasionally he would feel himself floating in a weightless, pink and green universe in which time had no meaning. Then there would be blank periods, hard black space, punctuated by vivid nightmares. Once he almost regained consciousness, and he dimly perceived plastic tubes sticking out of the veins in both arms.

Drugs.

It occurred to him in these periods of relative lucidity that they would be using a heavy concentration of scopolamine along with the Pentothal to enhance the nightmares. However, Chant knew all about drug therapy, and was confident that he was successfully resisting the questioning that took place while he floated in the pink and green sky. Since his captors would be well aware that they were unlikely to get what they wanted out of him with drugs, it occurred to Chant that he was being tentatively probed, softened up.

Of course, he was being transported out of Holland—illegally, through secret channels. The capture of the infamous international outlaw, John Sinclair, would have generated publicity around the world. Questions were certainly being asked, and although the CIA could do many things, they couldn't silence the Dutch police, Interpol, Bo Wahlstrom. Even as he was being slipped out of Amsterdam, Chant knew that there would be a flurry of increasingly loud questions about the whereabouts of the man called so many different things by so many different people—traitor and hero, vigilante and avenging angel of justice, mercenary and idealist, thief and philanthropist, terrorist and bringer of mercy, torturer and saint.

Many people would want to know where he was, but there would be no answers. The Americans who had him would resist all the pressures, deny they knew anything about him. And he would have disappeared, apparently be gone from the face of the earth. . . .

There was a sensation of flight—of many flights. Each time when he would drift toward consciousness he would feel the sharp sting of a needle slipping into his veins. More Pentothal and scopolamine, questions and his answers. Resist. Talk nonsense. He was conscious of time passing, but without any frame of reference he could not tell minutes from hours, days from weeks. There were only the drugs and the questions.

He did not tell them anything.

When he finally regained consciousness fully for the first time since being gassed in the bare cell in Amsterdam, he found himself in a straitjacket—the ties on the arms looped around and secured behind the straight-backed chair he was sitting in. His bare feet were tied to the chair legs. The chair had been placed in the center of a room with no windows. The table before him was bare except for a hand-cranked electrical generator. Cables from the generator's terminals snaked over the edge of the table and along the floor; the ends were clipped to Chant's left earlobe and his right ankle.

Sitting in the chair on the opposite side of the table was a portly man in a sweat-stained safari jacket worn over a grimy white shirt open at the collar. On his left cheek was a thin, purple birthmark that extended over his cheekbone to beneath one puffy lid. His eyes were mud-brown, cold, intelligent but cruel. They were the eyes of a hate-filled fanatic. Still. Thomas Maheu had changed little in twenty years, Chant thought. His hair had been dyed a chestnut color, but the too-bright eyes were still his main feature.

"Hello, Maheu," Chant said easily to the man who had once been responsible for overseeing all CIA covert operations in the entire region of Southeast Asia. "It's been a long time. How're tricks?"

"I finally got you, you son of a bitch traitor," the big man said in a hoarse, gravelly voice. "I always knew I would, sooner or later."

Chant yawned loudly. Maheu flushed, and his hand suddenly darted out and cranked the generator. Electricity flashed through Chant's body, seizing his muscles and bringing him up stiffly in the chair; a steel fist squeezed his heart, while fingers of pain pulled his testicles.

Then it was over. Maheu took his hand off the crank; the current stopped, and Chant slumped in the chair.

That was just a taste of what he was going to have to endure if he was to accomplish the task he had come here for, Chant thought. His agony was just beginning. Yet he had prepared his mind well, and he was ready. "You really light up my life, asshole," Chant said in the same easy tone. "I always knew you were an amateur in a job that was way too big for you. I'm really surprised they still let you hang around."

"I'll kill you, Sinclair."

"So kill me, and then you'll really put your ass in a sling. If you and the other big boys wanted me dead, I wouldn't be sitting here now, would I?"

Maheu's eyes clouded with frustration and rage. His fingers reached out and touched the wooden crank on the generator, but he did not turn it. "Where are they, Sinclair?"

Chant smiled. "Now, what on earth could you be talking about?"

"The Cooked Goose documents. You have files, affidavits from men you've talked to. I want to know where they are."

"It could be that the quickest way to find out where—and what—they are is to kill me. I don't know how much time has passed; maybe the files I have are on the way to newspapers right now."

"Don't try to bluff me, Sinclair. Nobody knows where you are now, and they're sure as hell unlikely to know when you die."

"My people know I was captured, you fat idiot. By now then know I'm missing, and they'll know you have me. Maybe they're waiting to hear from me, or maybe they'll automatically release the documents if I don't show up in a certain period of time."

"Which is it, you prick?"

"That's a good question, Maheu. Maybe you should just let me go."

"Did you say anything to Wahlstrom or the Dutch police?"

Chant laughed. "If I had, the whole world would know by now about Operation Cooked Goose, the plan that would have made the Bay of Pigs look like the ultimate exercise in sanity. No, Maheu. Keeping my secrets, having something to hold over your head and the others', is what's going to keep me alive."

"That's what you think, traitor. Everybody says you can't be broken, that you'll die before you talk." Maheu's voice was a sibilant, hoarse whisper of hate. "That's bullshit. I'll break you myself, and it's going to give me more pleasure than you can imagine. Because of you, *one man,* the United States lost that war."

"Jesus Christ, you really believe that?"

"I *still* believe it! I believed it then, and I believe it now!"

"That's because you've got shit for brains. You always did."

"Operation Cooked Goose would have worked!"

"If you're so certain about that, why be so concerned—even now, two decades later—that the American people are going to find out about the great plan you and a few others had cooked up, if you'll pardon the pun?"

"You know the answer to that, Sinclair. It could *never* be known, but it would have *worked!*"

"It would have torn the country right apart, idiot—possibly even have caused another civil war. You couldn't have kept something like that secret. Somebody would have been caught at it, or it would have leaked. The only good thing that would have come out of it would be the fact that you and those other creeps in the CIA and the Pentagon wouldn't still be in power. You were always a raving paranoiac, Maheu. You had to have been the principal architect of that quarter-assed plan, and you managed to dig up a few other raving paranoiacs in high positions of power to let you off the leash. *You're* the traitor, asshole, not me. In time, now that I've finally been forced into retirement, the truth is going to come out. I think you and I, the CIA, the Pentagon, and the world press are all going to have some interesting times ahead. You're finally going to get all the credit you deserve."

"Damn it, Sinclair, that would cripple the United States, and you know it! If that information ever comes out, we'll tear ourselves apart!"

"Hey, I just want to make sure you get the credit you deserve."

"Nothing about Cooked Goose is ever going to come out, Sinclair! You don't have any 'people' waiting on you; you play everything too close to the vest. You're a solo act—always have been. Anything you've got is sitting in a safe deposit box somewhere in the world, and you're going to tell me where."

"You could be right. Then again, you could be wrong. If you are, and you make a mistake, that information is going to come out, and one of us is going to join our country's Benedict Arnold shit list. Want to take bets who it will be?"

"Where are the documents, Sinclair?! What arrangements have you made?!"

"Why not try asking 'pretty please'?"

"I'll fry your fucking brains!" Maheu shouted, reaching for the crank on the generator, turning it slightly.

"Be my guest," Chant said through clenched teeth after the charge had ripped through his body. "Fry my brains, and you fry your ass. What are you now? You were a regional controller. You must have had quite a career setback after I took off, but you've obviously bounced back off the floor. What do you do now, Maheu? Director of Operations? Whatever you are and have, kiss it all goodbye if the truth about Operation Cooked Goose ever comes out. If this country survives it, your great-great-grandchildren will still be talking about it. You think they'll be proud of you, asshole?"

"You'll destroy the Company for sure!"

"If I wanted to destroy anything in the United States, I'd have done it long before now. You're the people who are pushing this, not me. It's your collective ass you're trying to save, not the Company's, and not the country's. But all will suffer. When those documents are finally released, and I think you know they will be, you and your buddies are going to be hanged by the balls. You're going to make the history books for sure, Maheu."

The words got the reaction Chant had been looking for; Maheu gripped the crank on the generator and began to turn it. An initial flash of pain became a white hot buzzsaw that ripped through his body. Maheu turned the crank even faster, and Chant knew that there was a very good chance that the other man, in his rage, would now kill him, regardless of the consequences. But he had wanted, needed, Maheu to begin cranking the electricity through him, for he needed the involuntary seizure of his muscles and spasmodic jerking of his body to cover what he was doing.

He used the ancient technique of *po-chaki* to seal a part of his consciousness away from the terrible pain; it was a mental sanctuary where he could, in effect, hide a small part of himself from agony for short periods of time, an eye in a hurricane of torment where he could marshal his *kai*, think, plan, and act. With *po-chaki*, a master could treat pain as no more than a temporarily distracting nervous sensation, almost a sister to pleasure, that was irrelevant to *kai*—power and purpose, the focusing of will. Actual physical damage was, of course, the real danger, and a very real possibility, but Chant could not do anything about that, and he dismissed it from his thoughts.

The electricity kept coming, coursing through him,

grinding his bones, wrenching his muscles, slamming him up and down in the chair. He could feel his heart palpitating, at the same time as he felt his joints popping, his stomach and bowels churning.

Still, Chant maintained his concentration in the pocket created by *po-chaki*. In the brief milliseconds between pulses of electricity he performed *satpi,* first dislocating both shoulders, then inching to his right, bringing one arm up over the back of the chair even as the electricity burned in him.

He lost *po-chaki* almost at the exact moment Maheu stopped cranking the generator, and Chant moaned and slumped forward, even as he brought his shoulder joints back into their sockets.

He had done what he had to do.

"*Any* man can be broken," Maheu said through clenched teeth. His jowled face glistened with sweat, and his safari jacket had turned a dark, stained brown. "You've caused me a lot of misery, and now I've returned the favor. I'm going to keep cranking this thing until you get smart. All you have to do to make me stop is to tell me what I want to know. I want to know exactly what you have on Cooked Goose, who you've talked to about it, where you've stored any records, and what arrangements—if any—you've made for having them released if you end up dead or missing."

Chant spat out the taste of vomit, slowly raised his head. Visible behind the sweating Maheu, the shocked face of a young man stared at him through an open porthole in the door. "All right," Chant said wearily, "let's talk."

"Good," Maheu grunted with obvious satisfaction as he leaned back in his chair and folded his hands on his protruding belly. "Let's hear what the legendary, indestructible John Sinclair has to say to his old boss."

"Well, old boss, do you remember what I did to that Ranger bodyguard of yours who came after me with a knife?"

Maheu frowned, unfolded his hands, and quickly leaned forward in his chair, causing the wood to groan. "You want more electricity, Sinclair?"

"I could have killed you then but, as you know, I needed you to deliver my message back to Langley. That was a long time ago. Now I don't need you as a messenger, so I'm going to do to you what I did to that Ranger."

Maheu's eyes went wide, the whites showing all around the pupils. He started to reach for the crank, and Chant tensed—but waited. Then Maheu abruptly jumped up, knocking over his chair, and stalked around the table. "You fucker! You want to play games with me?! I've been nice to you so far, but now I'm going to put those electrodes on the tip of your tongue and your prick. Five minutes from now, you won't be able to talk fast enough!"

Maheu slapped Chant hard, then reached for the electrode on his earlobe. He saw Chant make a slight shrugging and rocking motion, then gasped in astonishment as Chant brought his arms up over his head, freeing them. An instant later the laces on the arm restraints had been removed, the chair legs had been snapped with a flexing of Chant's knees, and the man with the iron-colored eyes and hair was standing before him. A hand shot out of the sleeve of the straitjacket, gripping Maheu's neck.

The nails of the middle and third fingers on both of Chant's hands were kept stone-hard by the regular application of special herbs, and always sharpened to a razor edge. Now these two nails on his right hand sliced easily into the flesh of Maheu's neck, next to the jugular. Chant thrust, twisted and pulled, tearing out the other man's throat. Blood spurted from the wound, spraying over Chant's face, then over the ceiling as Maheu toppled backward. Chant set the bloody remains of Maheu's throat on the table, then quickly shrugged out of the straitjacket.

The young guard who had been standing outside the door recovered from his initial shock and shouted. Then he flung open the door to the room and, closely followed by two other burly men in uniform, burst into the room and circled Chant, who found two submachine guns and a pistol equipped to fire tranquilizer darts aimed at his chest. Chant darted easily to one side, and a tranquilizer dart slammed into the wall behind him. Chant spun in the same motion, kicked one of the submachine-gun–carrying guards into the other. An instant later he had snatched their guns away. He walked up to the young man, who was standing watching Chant with his mouth open, and twisted the tranquilizer gun out of his grip.

Two more guards rushed into the room. Chant turned to them, smiled, then tossed both submachine guns to one side.

"Here," he said, picking up Maheu's bloody throat tissue and thrusting it into the startled young man's open palm. "Send me somebody else. This guy and I never got along well."

EIGHT

"I'M NOT AFRAID of you, Chant."

Chant casually crossed his legs over the edge of the cot, leaned back against the cold, brick wall of the cell, and folded his hands in his lap. "There's no reason you should be, Alan," Chant said easily to Lieutenant General Alan B. Steen, who was seated, feet flat on the floor and back stiff, on the cot across from him. There were no other prisoners in the huge Army stockade cellblock. Steen had sent Chant's guards away when he had entered the cell, and the door had been locked behind him. "I have no quarrel with you. You were always my friend. We fought some good battles together."

"This isn't a good battle you're fighting now, Chant."

"You could be right. Then again, you may not be in a good position to judge."

The black man with the large, sensitive black eyes smiled wanly. "And you could be right. Anyone who presumes to sit in judgment on Chant Sinclair is a fool. I would like to still consider you my friend."

"That's fine with me."

"You want coffee?"

"No, thank you."

"Sorry about what Maheu did to you. We didn't have anything to do with that, and we couldn't stop it."

"I know," Chant said casually to the man who had fought with him in Vietnam, and who, also doubling as a CIA operative, had trekked by his side through the forbidden jungles of Laos and Cambodia.

"We still can't," Steen said pointedly. "The infighting over who'd have jurisdiction if you were ever caught was settled ten years ago. Your ass belongs to the Company."

"I'm not worried about it."

Alan Steen smiled thinly. "How'd you do that to Maheu?" he asked, not bothering to try to hide his approval. "You were always just about supernatural when it came to the martial arts, but I've never heard of anybody being able to tear out another man's throat with his bare hands."

"It's just a trick."

"Who taught you those things, Chant?"

"Actually, a number of people."

"You won't tell me the names of any of them, will you?"

"No, it's not important."

Steen studied Chant for some time before speaking again. "The Company may think it is, Chant. There's been some thinking over the past few years that maybe you'd originally been trained in Russia—that maybe you'd always worked for the Soviets."

Chant merely laughed.

"How and where you were trained is one of the things they want to know, Chant," the black general said in the same serious tone.

"And you were sent to try the friendly approach?"

"Sure. Wouldn't you have been surprised if they hadn't sent someone who'd known you back in the war?"

"Sure. And you're a good choice. You're one of the most honest men I've ever met."

"I told them they were wasting their time."

"Still, I'm glad they sent you. I'm also glad to see that you're doing so well. It's not easy for somebody from the Regular Army who worked for the Company to move up in the ranks of either, and especially not easy for people who did the things we did, knew the things we knew."

Alan Steen shrugged. "I've been lucky."

"You're a damn good soldier—always were. Where are you stationed?"

"West Point. I'm Commandant."

Chant raised his eyebrows slightly. "I'm very impressed, Alan. Congratulations. Obviously, you're being groomed for very big things. I'm glad for you, glad for the Army, glad for the United States."

"You were never a part of Operation Cooked Goose, were you? You told Maheu to go fuck himself the first time he approached you on it."

Again, Chant raised his eyebrows slightly. "Is that what I did?"

"I know about Cooked Goose, Chant," Steen said quietly.

"What do you know about Cooked Goose?"

"I know all about it."

"That surprises me. If it's true, I'm sorry for you. It's an ugly secret, and the people who want to keep it hidden have a very nasty way of turning on you. I hope it doesn't cost you your career."

"They flew me in by private jet from the Point last night—after you'd disposed of Mr. Maheu. The CIA wanted somebody who'd been friends with you. I drew the assignment. The Company had to tell me everything; I insisted."

"Don't assume the Company ever tells you everything about anything. You know that."

"Sure. It doesn't matter. What matters is that you cut this shit out now and tell the Company what *they* want to know. The thing was a piece of shit, but I agree with them that *knowledge* of it, and what you could do with that knowledge, threatens the security of the United States of America. The game's over, Chant. Hang it up so they won't bust you up."

"Do you think I'd do anything to hurt this country's security, Alan?"

"I'm not sure," the general replied after a pause. "Always, even during the war, it was difficult to think of you as an *American,* in the sense that the rest of us were Americans. You were always . . . something else. I'm not sure I can explain it, or understand it myself, but there always seemed to be something inscrutable about you. One has the sense that you're incredibly loyal without knowing exactly what it is that you're loyal to. I can't say whether or not I feel sorry for you, Chant. Maybe I envy you for the freedom you enjoy as a kind of international samurai. But then, you're also a man without a country. I'm not sure how I feel about you, Chant."

"But you are sure you don't approve of what they wanted to do with Cooked Goose," Chant said dryly.

"I told you it was a piece of shit—an abomination. What's more, everyone I talk to who knows anything about it feels the same way."

"It's too bad they didn't express that disapproval twenty years ago. The Director of Operations himself, and one or two people on the the Joint Chiefs, must have approved it."

"Not the Joint Chiefs. It was a Company operation all the way."

"I should have found a way to kill the Director."

"He's dead."

"There may be people in Defense and State who were in on it."

"It's possible. I really don't know. All the evidence indicates that it was Maheu's original idea, and he ran hard with it."

"Maheu was responsible for the deaths of a lot of innocent people in Laos, Alan. He was after me."

"The record indicates that you killed a few people there yourself during your walk away from the war."

"Not innocents. Maheu sent assassins, Cooked Goose people, after me. This was after he'd killed about two dozen people who fought on our side, as well as my controller. Is that on the record?"

"No," Alan Steen replied quietly. "I didn't know that."

"Now you do."

Steen sighed. "It doesn't make any difference, Chant. We can't let you keep this thing hanging over us. Will you tell me what documents you have and where they're being kept?"

"No, Alan."

"Will you tell me anything?"

"I'll make a suggestion. The suggestion is, that while Cooked Goose may have been Maheu's original idea, which was approved by the Director of Operations, a number of other important people may have been consulted—Senators, Congressmen . . . maybe even a macho President."

"Impossible."

"If you say so. But it must seem strange to you that Maheu wasn't fired, or even assassinated. He had too much on too many people, and that's why he continued to move up in Company ranks. A lot of those people may still be in power, they may be respected elder statesman, or they may be dead and revered. Being tainted by a linking with Cooked Goose isn't going to do anyone any good. I was the last loose string—and I had to be cut off."

"Is it true, Chant? About all the others?"

Chant said nothing.

"Why won't you at least tell me that?"

"Because there's no point. The best thing is for the Company to simply let me go."

"That can't be, Chant."

"For twenty years, I said nothing and did nothing about Cooked Goose—despite the fact that the CIA was hunting my ass all over the world. It would be ironic if the truth about Cooked Goose came out now *because* they'd finally caught me, wouldn't it?"

"No man can be allowed that kind of power, Chant," Steen said with a shake of his head. "For one thing, there's always the danger than an enemy government might catch you and get the truth out of you. If the Russians ever got hold of those documents . . ." The general rose to his feet and began to pace back and forth along the length of the narrow cell. "We're all up to our ears in shit on this, Chant," he continued at last. "I'm not going to insult your intelligence by implying that I can bargain with you; I can't. There's nothing I can offer you. They're never going to let you go, my friend, because you're a little more than a loose string—you're a loose cannon, and always have been."

"This particular cannon's likely to blow up in everybody's face if I've made arrangements for those documents to be released in the event I disappear for a certain length of time, Alan."

Steen stopped pacing, and his dark eyes narrowed as he looked at Chant. "Obviously, that's been considered. The

Company's decided that it has no real choice except to proceed this way; it has you, and it's not going to let you go. They're going to get the information they want out of you, Chant. Believe it."

"Will they? Do they have another Maheu waiting in the wings?"

"Torture is not an official United States government policy, Chant, and you know it. The things that happened during the war were an aberration. Torture is expressly forbidden in all arms of the government, and you know that Maheu was acting on his own."

"The Company has a way of getting around those niceties."

"Damn right they do, and that's my point. I don't know what those spooks are planning for you, but I do know that they're absolutely confident they can break you. There's no way they can take a chance on you ending up in some foreign prison and writing your memoirs. Do you understand that, Chant?"

"I've always understood that."

"I believe them, Chant. I believe they can break even you. I don't know *how,* but I think it can happen. I don't want that. I can't offer you any kind of deal on behalf of anyone but myself. But I promise that, in return for your cooperation, I'll do everything in my power to see that the Company doesn't kill you. Nobody's ever going to hear of you again; that's for sure. But that doesn't mean that you can't be locked up someplace where it's reasonably comfortable. That's what I'll press for, although I can't promise anything. Will you cooperate, Chant?"

"No, Alan. But thanks for the offer."

The other man studied Chant for some time, then moved to the cell door. He stood with his hands gripping the bars, but did not call out to the guard. "There's something I don't understand," he said quietly, turning back to face Chant.

"What's that, Alan?" Chant asked, idly staring at the ceiling.

"All of the people who were approached to participate in Cooked Goose were carefully vetted as to attitude and political leanings beforehand. For example, I was never approached."

"Of course not. You were—and are—a soldier, not a political assassin. You'd have told Maheu the same thing I told him."

"Then whose idea was it to approach *you?*"

"Certainly not Maheu's," Chant said dryly.

"Then whose?"

Chant was silent for some time, a wry smile playing across his face. "An old enemy," he said at last.

"What?"

Chant looked at the other man. "When you were briefed on Cooked Goose, did they tell you that they'd brought in an outsider to act as a consultant and overall coordinator for the team they were trying to put together?"

Steen shook his head. "You were right, of course; never assume that the Company tells you everything about anything. Then again, the information may be classified beyond my—"

"Classified, bullshit," Chant said with a laugh. "It's been expunged."

"Who was this man?"

"A man who dealt in Black Flame," Chant replied, his voice suddenly distant.

"I don't understand."

"Neither did the Company. From the beginning, this man had foreseen what would happen if I ever found out about Cooked Goose. He was the one who insisted that

Maheu approach me and tell me about it."

"This man *wanted* the whistle blown on the very project he was supposed to coordinate?!"

"No, Alan. He wanted me killed. He guessed—correctly—that the Company would want me taken out as a security risk once I knew about Cooked Goose. The thought that I would finally be killed by my own people amused him."

"Your 'own people'? What was he?"

"He wasn't American."

"He was Japanese, wasn't he?"

"He wasn't American."

"*Who* was he, Chant?"

"One of my teachers you asked me about," Chant answered softly. "He was perhaps my greatest *sensei;* he was certainly the most evil, with a rather bizarre sense of humor. Forcing Maheu to tell me about Cooked Goose was his idea of an amusing, if deadly, practical joke."

"Why a joke?"

"You had to have known him, know the circumstances under which he became my enemy."

"What were the circumstances, Chant?"

Chant said nothing.

"Give me his name, Chant."

"No, Alan. It's not a name you'd want to know. More important, it's not a name the Company would want you to know. A warning, my friend. If you get too inquisitive, and don't watch your ass, you're likely to end up in the same situation I'm in. You've done what the Army and the Company wanted you to do; you've talked to me. Now walk away from it. Go back to West Point and forget any of this ever happened—hope that they leave you alone."

"Tell me, Chant," the general said, drawing himself up. "I want to know."

"Good-bye, Alan. Good luck."

Steen studied Chant, knew somehow that the other man would speak to him no more. He called to the guard, who came and opened the door. "Good-bye, Chant," he said quietly, then turned and walked away.

A half hour later they came to gas him.

NINE

THIS TIME CHANT awoke to find himself crucified on a cold stone wall, his wrists and ankles tightly gripped by shackles on chains that ran from sockets in the wall. He was cold, colder than he could ever remember being in his life. He was hungry, terribly thirsty. His breath misted in the frigid air as his cramped lungs struggled to draw in air, and the lower half of his naked body, like the stone floor below his feet, was covered with his own waste, involuntarily voided while he had been unconscious.

He sensed that the things he had brought with him were still in place, but they were irrelevant to his present situation; even had he wanted to get at them, he would not have been able to. There was nothing he could do but hang while his muscles cramped and his lungs labored, and he froze.

The cold numbed him. With an effort approaching desperation, Chant struggled to achieve, and remain in, a state of *po-chaki* during his periods of tormented consciousness, but the mental trance-state would not hold; each time it got smaller in space and time, shrinking under the constant onslaught of cold, hunger, and thirst. *Po-chaki* worked very well for enduring relatively brief periods of agony, but even this ancient, refined technique broke down under the incessant torture of crucifixion and freezing. His tongue seemed to swell, filling the back of his throat to choke him and make it even more difficult to breathe. Occasionally, mercifully, he would pass out.

Had he been left crucified for too long a period of time, he would have died as his lungs eventually collapsed under their impossible burden and he suffocated. On occasion, machinery behind the wall would rumble and the chains would loosen, snaking out from their steel sockets and gradually lowering him to the frigid stone of the cell floor. Exhausted, his resources drained, he would lie there in his own waste and desperately gasp for breath.

He must wait. He must wait. He must wait. What began as a silent refrain became a command. They did not mean to kill him—not yet. The cold, crucifixion, waste, hunger, and thirst were just a means of getting his attention before they started asking the inevitable questions.

He must wait.

Then, always just before he had quite caught his breath, the chains would retract into the wall, inexorably dragging him up and pinning him to the cold stone.

He began to pass out more frequently.

The next time he woke up, he found that he could breathe normally—and he was warm. Warm, citrus-scented water was falling over him in a fine spray from shower heads in the ceiling, washing down him and the cell, carrying his filth away into gutters gouged in the floor around the perimeter of the cell.

It was not a dream, Chant thought. He was awake, lying in his chains on the floor. He rolled on his back, opened his mouth, and drank deeply of the water pouring from the ceiling. His mind reeled. When he had drunk his fill, he collapsed, exhausted, on his side and let the water run over him, soothing his wrists and ankles where his shackles had rubbed the flesh raw.

He must wait.

The water abruptly stopped. Chant heard the heavy wooden door creak open, and he raised his head to see a man and woman carrying thick, Turkish towels shuffling toward him. Chant saw their half-naked bodies and groaned. It was impossible to judge their ages; both had snowy white hair, but what had been done to them would have whitened anyone's hair. Both the man and woman walked bent over, their shuffling, crablike steps made possible by heavy steel-and-leather braces on their legs. From the scars radiating from their knees, it appeared that the joints had been crushed, along with most of the other joints in their bodies. They were covered with scars. The eyes of both were very pale, as if their color had been washed out along with any reasons they may have had to live. In addition, both of the woman's breasts had been cut off.

"Who are you?" Chant asked in a thick voice as the broken man and woman shuffled up to him, laboriously lowered themselves to the floor, and began to gently towel him off.

There was no answer. Both sets of hollow, washed-out eyes avoided looking at him as the toweling continued.

"My God, did they do that to you here?"

There was still no answer. The man and woman finished

drying him off, then, holding on to each other for mutual support, struggled to their feet and shuffled out of the cell.

Almost immediately another broken man entered. Like the others, he could only walk with the aid of braces. In addition, he only had half a face; the other half looked as if it had been melted away, perhaps with acid. This man carried a tray, which he set down before Chant; on the tray were a tall glass and a frosted pitcher filled with an amber-colored liquid.

Chant tried speaking to this white-haired, broken man, but he was as mute as the others. After setting down the tray, he turned and walked away. Chant, sitting on a dry towel that had been left by the first couple, picked up the pitcher and sniffed at its contents; it was beer, ice cold. He poured himself a glass and sipped at it, shuddering with pleasure as the icy liquid flowed down his throat and into his stomach. He finished that glass, drank another. The light, salty taste of the beer stirred hunger pangs, and he wondered how long it had been since he'd eaten.

As if in response to his thought, the first couple reappeared. The woman carried a fresh pitcher of icy beer, and the man carried a tray that turned out to be stacked with sandwiches and fresh fruit. Chant looked at the food, at once feeling nauseous and dizzy as the aroma wafted into his nostrils. He half expected it to be snatched away when he reached for it, but it was not. The food was his. He forced himself to eat slowly, chewing carefully to get the maximum nutrition from the sandwiches and fruit, washing it down with glasses of beer.

Cigarettes, cigars, cognac, and a carafe of thick Turkish coffee were brought. Chant drank the coffee.

Without a word, the broken man and woman picked up the pitchers and tray and left the cell. As soon as they had disappeared from sight, Chant heard the machinery behind the wall begin to rumble. He barely had time to straighten out his limbs before he was dragged across the floor, lifted up, and pinned on the wall. Instantly, his heart began to hammer, his lungs to hurt. The fact that his belly was full and distended made him even more uncomfortable.

He was going to have to go on a diet if he stayed in this place much longer, Chant thought, and he allowed himself the luxury of a small smile.

His smile vanished when yet another man appeared in the open doorway. This man's hair was white like the others, but he walked upright and without the aid of braces. He was dressed all in white, from a tunic buttoned to the neck down to sneakers, and looked something like a hospital orderly.

The man appeared normal—except for his eyes, which were out of focus and glassy, as if the man were staring inward at some terrible nightmare from which he could not escape. His jaws were slightly slack, and a thin stream of saliva glistened in the fluorescent light as it ran down over his chin.

Chant sensed danger, and he instinctively tested his shackles; there was no play in them whatsoever.

"Uh, top of the morning," Chant said to the man. "What do you do here?"

The man in white smacked his lips, then stepped into the cell. Like some kind of insect fearing the light, he sidled around the wall, back pressed against the stone, unfocused black eyes directed toward Chant's belly. He came down the length of the cell, paused for almost a minute in the corner, then abruptly walked forward and stopped in front of Chant. Suddenly, without a sound, the man in white lunged forward and wrapped his arms around Chant's waist, locking his wrists at the base of Chant's spine.

Chant screwed his eyes shut, shook his head from side

to side, and groaned loudly in revulsion and pain as he felt the man's teeth sinking into the flesh of his stomach, just to the left of his navel. Chant bucked back and forth, trying to shake the man off him but the wristlock—and teeth—held him tight. The man bit deeper, working his teeth back and forth, gouging skin and muscle. White-hot pain flashed through Chant's stomach.

Then the man released his grip around Chant's waist and snapped his head back, tearing loose a bloody chunk of Chant's stomach. Chant's vision blurred, then came into focus again. He watched in horror that momentarily transcended his pain as the man gripped the ragged flesh with both hands, shoved it into his mouth and began to chew hungrily. With blood covering his white clothes, smeared over his mouth, chin, and the tip of his nose, the man slumped down in a corner, hunched his shoulders like some beast, and proceeded to enjoy the flesh.

Chant looked down at the wound in his stomach, which was bleeding profusely, sending rivulets of warm blood down into his groin and onto his legs to drip off his toes onto the stone below his suspended feet. The bleeding would be good if it did not last too long, Chant thought, for it would cleanse the wound. On the other hand, such thoughts might well be irrelevant.

The man in white had chewed and swallowed the flesh, and was hungrily eyeing Chant's stomach once again. He slowly rose to his feet and came forward, mouth open showing bloody teeth, arms outstretched to grab and grip. . . .

Like Harry, Chant thought as he bucked helplessly on the wall, he was going to be eaten alive.

Suddenly, from somewhere out in the corridor, a shrill whistle blew. The man in white stopped as suddenly as if he had suddenly come up against an invisible wall. His strange, unfocused eyes rolled in fear, then he wheeled and sprinted from the cell, turning right and immediately disappearing from sight.

A few moments later a tall, rangy man with carefully cut, shoulder-length yellow hair strode purposefully into the cell, the heels of his polished black shoes clicking on the stone. He wore a white coat over a white shirt and tie, black slacks. A stethoscope hung around his neck. The man stopped a few feet away from Chant, studied the crucified body with eyes that were a very pale green, almost white. Then he averted his gaze and made a few notes on a clipboard he carried with him.

A sizable retinue trailed into the cell after him, stopped, and crowded together at the opposite end, a respectable distance away from the new man in white who stood below Chant. Chant counted a dozen men, some in different types of uniforms and others in ill-fitting civilian clothes, who he assumed were the facility's current crop of "guest torturers." He recognized one of the faces, and the close-set, beady eyes of this slight man glared at Chant with open hatred. Although it was not warm in the cell, sweat poured off the man's face.

There were also five men dressed in brown slacks and brown T-shirts, wearing revolvers in holsters hanging at their hips. The man below Chant stopped writing on his clipboard and, without looking around, casually snapped his fingers. One of the brown-uniformed guards, a heavy-set man who nonetheless moved with an easy grace, stepped forward. The man carried a black leather satchel, which he set down at the other man's feet. All the while, his gaze remained on Chant—defiant, challenging. When Chant did nothing but casually return his gaze, the burly man stiffened, took a step back, and clenched his fists at his sides. He wore his hair in a crewcut, and the fluorescent light made his scalp beneath the sandy hair glow pink.

The man with the stethoscope handed his clipboard to the burly guard, then opened the satchel and removed sponges, gauze pads, and what appeared to be a bottle of antiseptic.

"Dr. Richard Krowl, I presume," Chant said easily as the white-coated man began to work on the bite wound, stanching the flow of blood, cleansing it.

"How do you like it here, Mr. Sinclair?" the man replied without looking up from the wound, his conversational tone matching Chant's.

"It's not Club Med."

"Did you expect to wake up in Club Med?"

"On the other hand, there's never a dull moment. You never know what's going to happen next."

"Mmmm." The man with the pale green eyes and long yellow hair finished cleansing the wound, then quickly and expertly closed the wound with four stainless steel butterfly clips. Only then did he look up. "I suppose you find this whole experience upsetting."

"I try to keep an open mind. After all, I'd had my dinner, so I suppose your resident cannibal had to have his. Have you considered putting him on a vegetarian diet?"

"Ah, you should have suggested that to his former captors," Krowl said as he again dipped into his bag and removed a shiny syringe filled with clear liquid. "In the course of the rather lengthy and inefficient interrogations this man and his comrades underwent, human flesh—each other's—was all there was to eat. It drove him quite mad, and I'm afraid he developed a rather exclusive taste for it. After I found out what they wanted to know, I found it useful to keep him around."

"He certainly does add local color."

Krowl smiled faintly. He carefully balanced the syringe over the open edges of the satchel top, then proceeded to probe and explore Chant's musculature with his fingers, tapping, thumbing, probing, occasionally stopping to listen to Chant's heart and lungs with the stethoscope.

He was good, Chant thought, with an expert—even gentle—touch. It was precisely the skill betrayed by the gentle touch that could cause exquisite, prolonged agony. Chant had seen one example of Richard Krowl's skills—keeping Harry Gray alive for weeks while his body was destroyed in the most brutal manner imaginable. But, as Gerard Patreaux had pointed out, Krowl had been sending a message. Chant suspected that the torture doctor was quite capable of delivering as much agony in ways that were more . . . creative.

Chant looked up and stared impassively back at the faces that were staring at him. Chester Norham, slight and sickly-looking even in his American Nazi uniform, was the only one Chant recognized, although he suspected he had crossed the paths of many of the men in the room. Norham was also the only one who looked either slight or sickly; the others fit a pattern Chant had come to recognize, despite their different nationalities—some, like the Greek, were brutish, while the Korean and the South Americans were more slender. But all had the same rather glazed eyes of men with low intelligence whose only real pleasure in life, pleasure inextricably linked in their minds with sex, was the domination of others and the inflicting of pain. The brown-uniformed guards were the same.

Chant wondered what Chester Norham was doing on Torture Island, how this joke of an American Nazi from Chicago had even heard of the place, much less arranged an invitation and the necessary financing to make the trip. He also wondered if the pimply-faced man had dared to pack his collection of women's underwear in his suitcases.

Chant also wondered about Richard Krowl. The man displayed much more than the rudimentary skills possessed by most torture doctors. He appeared to be highly intelligent, and even displayed some wit, macabre though it might be. Krowl was not exactly what Chant had expected.

Krowl finished his physical examination, picked up the syringe and shot a fine stream of fluid into the air. "I'm giving you a tetanus shot. We certainly wouldn't want you to get an infection."

"Thanks," Chant said dryly. "I was really worried about that."

"What is this nonsense the CIA wants to know about a cooked goose?" Krowl asked as he slid the needle directly into the wound and pressed the plunger.

"Cooked who?"

A deep, rumbling voice, speaking English with a heavy Greek accent, suddenly came from the back, grating in the relatively still, almost eerily normal conversational atmosphere in which Chant and Krowl had been engaging in their initial test of courage, wits, and will.

"I would not give this smear of scum a shot; I would crush his fucking balls until he told me what I wanted to know."

Krowl's reaction was immediate and explosive. He yanked the syringe from Chant's side and threw it against the wall, smashing the glass tube. His face crimson with rage, he wheeled and, long yellow hair flowing back, strode quickly down the length of the cell, pushing his way through the startled group members until he was face-to-face with the offending man—a swarthy Greek with sloped shoulders and a pot belly. Without hesitation, the tall torture doctor reared back and slapped the man across the face with such force that the sound of the blow reverberated in the stone cell. Blood spurted from the Greek's split lip. His eyes went wide with shock, which quickly turned to rage. His face mottled with blood, he started to reach for Krowl's throat.

Instantly, the five brown-uniformed guards leapt forward to surround the Greek. The burly, quick man with the crewcut reached out and gripped the Greek's wrist in the air, effortlessly held it there while the flesh beneath his fingers went white. Now fear moved in the man's dark eyes, and he began to sweat.

"Never speak to a prisoner without my permission, Colonel," Krowl said, his voice quivering with cold fury. "Not to, and not in front of. *Never!* Do you understand?!"

"You go too far, Krowl!" the Greek snapped back. "Tell this man to release my wrist!"

"Bernard will break your wrist if I tell him to, Colonel. You came here to *learn,* you fool. This facility is staffed by a score of men and women with broken bodies that fools like you produced, and then had to be sent to me when your methods didn't produce results. You fools don't understand anything. Now, Colonel, the helicopter will be here in a week. If you *ever* interfere again like this with a prisoner, I'll have you locked up in your room until the helicopter comes. I'll tell your employers that you're too stupid to learn anything. Who knows? They might send you back to me as a test subject. Would you like that, Colonel?"

The swarthy colonel averted his eyes, shook his head. "No, Dr. Krowl. I wouldn't like that."

"Release him, Bernard."

The burly American with the crewcut released the Greek's wrist. The colonel rubbed his wrist, stepped back against the wall, and stared sullenly at the floor. Krowl looked around at the other faces, took a deep breath, then slowly walked back toward Chant. He stopped a few paces away, once again turned around to face the others.

"All of you are here for one specific purpose," the torture doctor continued evenly. "You are here to learn how to extract information from unwilling subjects who may well be tougher, cleverer, and more devious than you are. You must begin to look upon pain as one of many tools, not as an end in itself. You didn't need to come here to learn to torture for punishment or vengeance—all of you certainly have enough experience at that. While you're here as my guests, you will follow my instructions to the letter." Krowl paused, sighed, and rested his hands on his hips. "Are there any comments or questions on this policy?"

Krowl waited. When he was met by nothing but silence, he turned around to face Chant, a small smile of satisfaction on his face.

"Good classroom control, Doctor," Chant said. His lungs hurt and the muscles around his rib cage were beginning to cramp, but he managed to keep his voice steady.

Krowl grunted. "What terrifies you most, Mr. Sinclair? Castration? Blinding? Having your tongue cut out? How would it be if I cut off your arms and legs and made you into the ultimate basket case? I could hang you up as a decoration."

Chant pretended to think about it, sniffed. "I can't say any of those choices really appeal to me. I hope that's not your only list."

"Lesson number one," Krowl said in the same even tone, turning back to face the guards and torturers. "Terror is what makes a subject talk, and terror is a function of the mind, not the body. Pain, of course, feeds terror, but the human nervous system can be overloaded with pain much easier and quicker than any of you in this room think. It is the *anticipation* of pain that eats away at the soul and breaks the will. Whatever is done to the subject, it is most important that the subject believe that there are *worse* things that can happen. *Terror,* not the heated tong, is your most important ally when it comes to extracting accurate information from men or women who are very strong, perhaps trained to resist torture, and who fully expect to die. They *want* to die. Remember that. Certainly, in many of these cases, they prefer death to revealing secrets that will cost the lives of mothers, fathers, their children. You begin breaking a body that is thirsting for the peace of death, and that body can die very quickly. I'm sure all of you have had that experience."

There were a few murmurs of assent. Krowl nodded, pointing back at Chant.

"Take the man hanging on this wall as a case in point," Krowl continued. "He displays extraordinary emotional control, is defiant, and even makes jokes about his situation. However, what he says and how he *seems* to react to pain, threats, and graphic suggestions as to what may be done to him isn't important. It's his *mind* that must be worked on; his mind, his terror, is your ally, and this man's mind is now beginning to work against him. Remember that your prisoner is under your absolute control, so there's no need to be impatient. Think of the human mind and body as making up one complex musical instrument. Learn to play it skillfully, and you will almost always, eventually, hear the music you want.

"Taking care to make certain that *your* behavior is unpredictable is of utmost importance. The nervous system is like a taut bowstring that will lose its resilience if it is *constantly* mistreated; the subject will feel pain, for sure, but his experience of that pain will not be maximized unless the nervous system is operating at full capacity. For example, when the subject is tortured to the point of unconsciousness, the bowstring may be said to have gone slack. The string must be kept taut. You do this by occasionally interrupting pain with pleasure—warmth instead of heat, food, water, cigarettes; occasionally no more than a kind word or expression of sympathy can break a man where nothing else had seemed to work. The subject must never be able to predict which he will get at any given moment—pain or pleasure. The pleasure restores resiliency to the string you wish to pluck, and the unpredictability feeds terror."

A hand was raised. Like a patient schoolmaster, Krowl, hands clasped behind his back, walked up to the man, bent forward as the questioner whispered in his ear. He nodded, then returned to the spot where he had originally been standing.

"The question has been raised as to why I tip my hand, so to speak, in front of the prisoner. The answer is that there is nothing I can say to you that John Sinclair does not already know. He is fully aware of what I'm doing, of the techniques I have used, and will use on him. It doesn't make any difference; despite the demeanor he presents to you, I can assure you that he's terrified. The face he presents to you is an illusion; reality will be reflected in the fact that his pulse rate will be well over a hundred and ten."

Krowl beckoned to the man he had called Bernard, who came forward and picked up the clipboard. As Bernard waited with a pencil poised over the paper on the board, Krowl put the plugs of his stethoscope into his ears, stepped forward and placed the steel listening plate against Chant's chest. He listened for a few moments, moved the stethoscope a few inches and listened again. Then he abruptly stepped back, snatched the plugs from his ears and glanced up at Chant. Uncertainty and consternation flickered briefly across the surface of his pale green eyes, but was quickly masked from Chant's inquiring and vaguely bemused gaze.

"What's the prognosis, Doctor?" Chant asked, raising his eyebrows slightly.

Bernard started to say something, but Krowl cut him off with a curt gesture. He snatched the clipboard out of the other man's hand, scribbled something over the top sheet, then dropped the board into his satchel. A questioning murmur arose from the group of onlookers.

He wasn't the only one on this island with a problem, Chant thought as he looked out at the torturers, many of whom now appeared openly disdainful and skeptical. Krowl had humiliated one of their number, and now Krowl found himself with a problem of credibility before an audience he had chosen to alienate and make hostile. The result was that two camps had been created—the body crushers against the soul crusher—and Chant immediately began to consider ways in which he might exploit this division.

Krowl cleared his throat. "Always there is terror," he said to no one in particular, then turned and looked up at Chant. His lips formed a tight smile. "Well, Mr. Sinclair," the torture doctor continued in a lighter tone, "it seems you're a celebrity. I'd never heard of you, but it seems that almost all of my distinguished guests have. You've enjoyed quite a career; you've moved around a great deal, and have caused considerable distress to a great many people."

"I'm afraid I only recognize one friendly face," Chant replied, looking out over the torturers and guards. "Hey, Chester, how's your mother?"

The slight man in the Nazi uniform shuffled his feet nervously, and his face reddened. The others moved a few steps away, leaving him isolated. Chester Norham stood glaring at Chant, his face blood red, his hands trembling.

"Go," Krowl said quietly to Chester Norham, who abruptly turned and walked stiffly from the cell.

"Where the hell did you find him, Krowl?" Chant said dryly. "You give scholarships?"

"Pay attention, please," Krowl said as angry murmurs arose from the torturers. "For those of you who don't know, that man is here at the behest of one of your countries. Your political affiliations and affections don't interest me; financing a cretin like that represents a mistake in judgment on your part, not mine. What is of interest here is the fact that Mr. Sinclair was able to play off his knowledge of that man to distract, divide, and disrupt. Already, some of you are beginning to question my methods and my handling of this particular subject. In effect, you have been given a most artful demonstration of precisely *why* the secrets locked up in John Sinclair's mind would remain a mystery to all of you right up to the moment when you squashed the last life out of him. Ponder that point, gentlemen."

Richard Krowl abruptly wheeled around, stepped up to Chant, and again began probing his body with his fingers. This time his deft, expert touch sought and found sensitive nerve bundles. Chant willed himself to be still, and silent, under the torture doctor's knifelike stabs.

"However," Krowl continued evenly as he stepped back and motioned for Bernard to step forward, "there are times when the simple application of brute force as punishment is appropriate. This is such a time. Bernard, please give Mr. Sinclair a demonstration of your skills."

Chant went deep into himself, focusing his concentration and *kai* in the center of his body as the man with the sandy hair and gleaming scalp bounced a few times on the balls of his feet, then went down into a karate fighting stance. One of his feet shot out in a side kick, landing on Chant's stomach a few inches to the right of the bite wound. Chant used his *kai* to absorb the blow, diffuse its force. Despite the tremendous shock of the blow absorbed by his body, his face revealed nothing. Even as the *thud* of flesh against flesh echoed in the chamber, Chant gazed impassively back at Bernard.

The American blinked in disbelief, took a step backward. His face darkened with blood and his eyes clouded with rage. He uttered a sharp cry, leapt forward, and slammed his fist against Chant's ribs.

That was the last blow his *kai* could absorb, Chant thought. The American did more than strike many poses. He knew his karate, and he was good; the foot and hand blows had been focused and powerful. At the next one, his bones would begin to break.

Still, Chant's face revealed nothing.

"Enough, Bernard!" Krowl snapped as the other man, enraged, began to wind up for a roundhouse kick that might have crushed Chant's thigh, chest, or skull.

For a moment Chant thought Bernard might ignore the command and fire his kick. But he didn't. Still trembling with rage, his dark brown eyes smoldering with hate and humiliation, he relaxed his body and stepped back.

"You are quite a remarkable man, Mr. Sinclair," Krowl said easily, staring up at Chant. Now there was a new element in his voice and eyes. There was respect—and quickening interest. "Often, the reputations of subjects who come under my care are overblown, magnified by the emotions of the authorities who have failed to deal with them successfully. You may be an exception. Perhaps many of the things these gentlemen say and believe about you are true. I must say that I've read your dossier with minimal attention, and listened to the stories with half an ear. That will no longer be the case. It's beginning to appear that you will make a most interesting subject. There may be much I can learn from you."

Chant wanted to say something, but he was no longer certain of his control so he remained silent. His face, however, remained impassive, revealing nothing of his terrible exhaustion and suffering.

At a signal from Krowl, the torturers and guards began to file out of the cell. The Greek colonel was the last to leave. The heavyset man with the dark, swarthy complexion stopped in the doorway, turned back to face Chant, and mouthed the words: *I would crush your balls*.

Chant blew him a kiss.

TEN

A HALF HOUR later the chains came out from the wall, allowing him to lie on the floor, breathe normally, and rest his severely cramping muscles.

He must wait.

The respite lasted less than fifteen minutes. Then the machinery rumbled, the chains retracted, and Chant was pulled back up to be crucified on the stone wall.

Although there were no windows in the cell, and the fluorescent lights were always on, he found that he was able to tell day from night by the relative brightness in the corridor outside the small porthole in the heavy wooden door. It was night.

A key rattled in the lock. The door abruptly swung open, and a figure in a flowing, cowled green robe glided almost silently into the cell. The figure, face hidden in the deep folds of the cowl, stopped before Chant and stared up at him for some time.

"Is it Halloween?" Chant asked.

Delicate hands with long fingers emerged from the heavy sleeves of the robe, reaching up and pulling back the cowl. Chant found himself looking down into the face of one of the most beautiful women he had ever seen. He put her age at around thirty, and her almost translucent olive skin and rich, black hair made him think that she was South American, perhaps Brazilian or Colombian. Her black eyes were large and beautiful, yet oddly blank—as if they were one-way mirrors behind which she was hiding and watching him; although her face was beautiful, and her hair was dark black and flowing, the eyes were like those of the broken people who had come to Chant.

The woman undid the sash around her waist and shrugged. The robe slid off her shoulders to the floor, and she stepped out of it to stand a short distance away from him, the firm nipples of her bare breasts just touching the flesh above the hair of his genitals. His skin fluttered from the touch of the nipples, and Chant heaved a sigh as he stared down into the vacant face.

"All appearances to the contrary," he said wryly, "I'm betting that you are definitely not an angel of mercy."

The woman stepped back a pace, reached into the back pocket of her skintight leather pants and drew out a large, snow-white feather that was more than a foot long. Holding the end of the thick, colorless shaft with her right hand, she used the long fingers of her left to smooth the feather. Her face remained blank as she continued to stare vacantly at a spot just above Chant's navel.

'Who are you?" Chant asked, feeling increasingly uneasy.

The woman's response was to reach out and begin to lightly stroke Chant's body with the tip of the feather, concentrating on the lower belly and the swollen flesh around the clamped bite wound. Chills ran up and down Chant's body, making his stomach and thigh muscles flutter spasmodically, giving him both pain from the increased cramping, and pleasure; her use of the feather had a curiously anesthetic effect, and the sharp, stinging sensation in the bite wound had disappeared.

Without warning, the woman reversed the feather in her hand and jabbed the hard, thick end of the shaft into his lower belly, just above the diaphragm where the stomach muscles are weakest. She kept pressing with the feather until it felt as if the shaft would pierce the skin, and he could no longer breathe. Pain burned in the spot where she pressed, radiating up into his heart and lungs. His vision blurred.

Just when Chant thought he would pass out, the woman suddenly released the pressure. His breath exploded from his lungs, and he gulped air. She again reversed the feather and began to stroke the spot on which she had been pressing. The pain disappeared.

Then she started on his face, brushing the feather across his eyes, around his nostrils and ears, under his chin, up and down his throat. The stroking continued with almost monotonous, hypnotic regularity until he was suddenly jabbed with the shaft end in the jugular. A lump of fire filled his throat and exploded into slivers of pain that shot through his head and down his spine.

Then the gentle stroking was resumed, easing his pain, making it possible for him to once again swallow.

The woman knew what she was doing, Chant thought, and she was very good. He considered her more dangerous, in her way, than the torturers who had been in his cell earlier. There was no doubt in his mind that the woman knew the human body extremely well, and was a master of the strange weapon she wielded; she was a woman who could literally, over a period of time that for him would be a hellish eternity, crush him with a feather.

Using the feather to stroke his buttocks, the backs of his knees and the base of his spine, the woman pressed her cheek against the inside of his thigh and licked his stiff penis while at the same time gently running her fingertips up and down its length and beneath his testicles.

Chant burned with desire under the controlled caresses of the feather, tongue, and fingertips, the warm touch of her lips, on his flesh. The woman with the feather was his most dangerous tormentor, Chant thought; she was systematically eroding, wearing away, his inner controls. He understood what was happening, knew that every second of pleasure would be paid for with many seconds of agony. Yet he did not want her to stop. The creation of this ambivalence, Chant knew, was an important step in a process that could break him.

The woman ran the feather up and down the insides of his thighs, and around the tip of his penis. Then she took him into her mouth.

Chant knew he should seek a way to resist, to at least kill his sexual desire, but he could not. He could feel his passion growing like a beast with a mind of its own. Pressure continued to build in his groin as her mouth moved up and down on his stiff shaft. Even as he felt himself getting ready to ejaculate, he knew that agony would be his very soon; he simply did not know what form it would take.

Suddenly the woman drew her head back and wrapped her thumb and forefinger tightly around the base of his penis, trapping the blood in the engorged erectile tissue; he would not lose his erection until she released her grip.

Then she unhurriedly went to work on the sensitive tip with the shaft of her feather. Chant screamed, and kept screaming until finally he passed out.

• • •

He regained consciousness to find the woman standing before him, mute and vacant-eyed as before, patiently waiting. Seeing that Chant was awake, she began all over again.

The session lasted through the night; it was the longest night of Chant's life, a seemingly endless tapestry of alternating agony and ecstacy. The woman never allowed him to release sexual tension through ejaculation, but always seemed to know the split second when he was ready. This, when his nervous system had been stimulated to its peak, was when the agony would begin. On this night Chant, who had been shot, burned, and electrocuted, experienced the worst pain he had ever known.

As dawn was seeping into the corridor outside the cell, he screamed and passed out once again.

ELEVEN

THIS TIME HE awoke to find himself dressed in a blue, loose-fitting jumpsuit and strapped into a wheelchair, his wrists and ankles held firmly in place by rigid steel cuffs. He looked around the cell, found that he was alone. His body, from the top of his head to the soles of his feet, throbbed with pain, and there was a constant burning, bruised sensation in his groin. He was exhausted and, he knew, near the end of his resources, both mental and physical.

Still, he must wait. In any case, he did not seem to have a choice at the moment.

He tensed the muscles in his arms and legs in order to test the strength of the steel cuffs, and immediately felt electricity course through his body. He stiffened and jerked in the chair under the onslaught of the electricity. After a few seconds there was a clicking sound from beneath the chair, and the electricity stopped. Chant slumped in the chair and waited, at the same time trying to take a mental inventory of how much damage had been done to him by the woman with the feather. He decided that there was indeed damage, but not permanent injury. He closed his eyes and concentrated on marshaling his resources, focusing his strength and banishing his anxiety over what might be waiting for him at the end of the journey he appeared about to take in the wired wheelchair.

He opened his eyes when he heard a key rattle in the lock. The heavy door swung open and Bernard, carrying a tray, sauntered into the cell, leaving the door open behind him. Once again, Chant was impressed by the lithe, easy way the big man with the bullet head moved.

Bernard sat down on the floor, his back against the wall. With the tray resting in his lap, he began to eat. The redolent aroma of bacon, eggs, potatoes, toast, and coffee drifted into Chant's nostrils, momentarily making him dizzy with hunger.

"How'd you like your session with Feather, tough guy?" Bernard rasped around a mouthful of food. Egg yolk dripped down his chin, and he wiped it away with the back of his hand. "She do a job on your pecker?"

Chant licked his cracked lips, then swallowed to work up some saliva. "Actually," he said in a voice that was firm, "I found her a bit kinky. Not quite to my taste."

"Man," Bernard said absently as he shoveled more food into his mouth, "I'd like to fuck the brains out of that spooky broad. That'd fix her good. Problem is, there ain't nothing left down there to fuck. I wouldn't trust her with my prick in her mouth; she might bite it off."

Chant frowned at the words, studied the other man. "My goodness, Bernard," he said at last, his light tone belying the unease he had felt at the man's description of the woman he'd called "Feather," "how can you call that lovely young lady 'spooky'? Now, *you* I call spooky."

Bernard looked up sharply, and his brown eyes glinted. "Watch your mouth, Sinclair. Try to get smart with me, and I'll—!"

"Uh-uh, Bernard. Control your temper. If you'd been sent over to beat up on me, I wouldn't be sitting here in this wheelchair in my Sunday finest, and you wouldn't be slouched over there feeding your fat face. My guess is that the good Dr. Krowl wants you to do nothing more than wheel me to him. You know how upset he gets when his flunkies don't obey his orders."

"Fuck you, Sinclair!" the big man shouted, leaping to his feet and kicking over the tray, spilling the rest of his food over the floor.

"Dear me," Chant said, "I've ruined your breakfast. Sorry if I seem a bit cranky, but I got up on the wrong side of the bed this morning. I can't stand to see someone in a good mood when I'm not."

There was some truth in what he said, inasmuch as Bernard had seemed too comfortable and self-confident. Although he knew there was considerable risk in goading Bernard while he himself was helpless, strapped in the wheelchair, it was a calculated risk he felt he must take. He wanted his enemies upset, at each other's throats if he could manage it, enraged at him if that was the only alternative. An enraged enemy was a less-than-attentive, weakened enemy. At the moment, his mind and his mouth were his only weapons.

Bernard kicked the wheelchair, causing the contacts beneath Chant's wrists and ankles to close, jolting him with electricity from the battery mounted beneath the seat.

"Thanks, you chickenshit bastard," Chant said when the automatic cutoff had stopped the electrical current and he was able to speak again. "I needed that."

Bernard glared, bared his teeth. "I ain't chickenshit, Sinclair, and I ain't Richard's flunky. If I had my way, I'd have beat the truth out of you the minute you arrived. My brother ain't as goddam smart as him and everybody else thinks he is, and I ain't as stupid."

"Krowl is your brother?"

"Yeah."

"Shit. I don't know which one of you I feel more sorry for."

Bernard's voice grew oddly hushed, and Chant sensed that the man was struggling with old wounds and resentments. "My brother's got his own way of doing things; that makes him stupid, and it makes you lucky. He's still trying to prove something to those bastards who threw his ass out of med school. I ain't got nothing to prove to anybody. I know I'm a better man than he is, and I'm a better man than you are. I don't give a shit about your reputation."

Chant cocked his head and studied the other man, whom he judged to be in his late twenties or early thirties, a few years younger than Richard Krowl. "My reputation really bothers you, doesn't it, Bernard?"

"You know, I didn't hit you as hard as I could have. You ain't as tough as all these people think you are, and you ain't as tough as you think you are."

"How tough do all of us think I am?"

"Like I said, you got the reputation. But nobody can do all the things you're supposed to be able to do. All these dumb fucks my brother brought here are afraid of you, but I ain't. Some of them say you're the best martial arts expert in the world, and I say that's bullshit."

"Of course it's bullshit," Chant replied mildly, intrigued by the huge man's almost childlike need to bluff and boast. "The best are never heard of."

"Damn right it's bullshit," the child-man said, thumping

his chest. *"I'm* the best. I was world PKA champion. I still would be if the candy-ass pricks who run things hadn't barred me from fighting after I killed a guy in the ring."

"Oh, my."

Bernard grinned. "They said I was too wild."

"It wasn't an accident, was it, Bernard?"

"Fucking right, it was no accident—the same as it was no accident when I killed those niggers when I was a cop in Chicago. Guys like you and my brother get all the breaks, and that's how you get your reps. I was too young for 'Nam, Sinclair, but if I'd fought over there I'd have won all the medals people say you won." The man with the crewcut and pinkish scalp paused, frowned slightly. "Did you really win the Congressional Medal of Honor twice?"

"What do people say?"

"I'd have won it, Sinclair. Those people who give the tests don't know what they're talking about when they say I'm not smart enough. Shit, I'd have killed more fucking gooks than all the rest of the army put together."

"You don't know all the fun you missed, sonny. I'll bet those Vietnamese up in Ho Chi Minh City are still breathing sighs of relief that you weren't old enough to have won the war for us."

"With the right breaks, I would have had your rep, Sinclair. I can do all the things you're supposed to have done. You ain't such a tough shit."

Chant yawned loudly. "Sonny, you're a chickenshit flunky who's lucky his big brother had a job for him on this island beating up on people who can't fight back. This is probably the only job you've ever held for more than a week."

Bernard flushed. "You don't know what the fuck you're talking about, Sinclair. It's *Richard* who's lucky I'm here. Because of me, he's going to be a rich man. Ain't nobody else around here got the guts to do what I do."

"What do you do for him, flunky? You shit black pearls?"

Bernard frowned, and his eyelids narrowed. "How do you know about the black pearls?"

"Some people have heard of me, and I've heard of your brother. The story is that he has a fortune in them."

"Thanks to *me*, he has a fortune in them. *Half* a fortune. Half are mine. He may not give a shit about them now, but he will when he gets all this research crap out of his system."

"What research?"

Bernard bared his teeth, laughed. "When Richard gets through with you, you'll go to the shacks. Then, when I feel like it, I'll give you a demonstration of how I get the pearls." He paused, laughed again. "You'll be my helper, Sinclair. *Then* we'll see who's chickenshit."

"Where are the pearls, Bernard? Where do you keep them?"

"What the hell do you want to know that for?"

Now it was Chant's turn to laugh. "Christ, Bernard, you *are* stupid. I plan to steal them, of course, and I can't do that unless I know where they are. Why else would I ask? For that matter, why else would I come to this lovely resort?"

Shadows moved in Bernard's eyes, and he shook his head slightly. "You're crazy, Sinclair."

"Maybe the stories about the black pearls are just bullshit. If you claim that you get them and that it takes guts, then it must be bullshit."

Bernard was about to reply when the small beeper he carried in his shirt pocket sounded. A moment later Richard Krowl's voice, tinny on the tiny speaker, could be heard.

"Bring him now, Bernard. I'm ready."

Chant smiled. "It seems I was right. Let's go, flunky. We don't want to keep big brother waiting."

Bernard flushed a deep crimson. He reached into his pocket to shut off the beeper, then stepped around behind the wheelchair. "Fuck him," Bernard said through clenched teeth as he shoved Chant forward. "And fuck you, too. I'll show you bullshit, Sinclair."

TWELVE

THE MASSIVE AMERICAN wheeled Chant out of the cell and to the left, down a long concrete corridor past cells that were similar to Chant's, but which were empty. At the end of the corridor a ramp, obviously designed for wheelchairs, sloped gently upwards. Chant was pushed up the ramp, through a set of salon-type swinging doors, to emerge in bright sunlight.

Chant drank in the fresh, salty air, taking it deep into his lungs, renewing his strength. There was a stiff breeze blowing in from the west, and it whipped his overalls, snapping the material with a sound like small-arms fire. He was wheeled up a sidewalk to a small, concrete square where other walks branched off in four different directions. Bernard spun him around, pushing him down the walk that had been on their extreme left.

Now Chant could see that the cellblock where he had been imprisoned was a long, low concrete building set on the very edge of an escarpment that was a sheer drop to the sea. The route Bernard was taking led along the very edge of that escarpment, the rim of the island, and Chant could glance down to his left and see the ocean, three hundred feet below, cascading furiously against, over, and around coral reefs in a crashing maelstrom of foaming death. Far in the distance, he could just see the peaks of the Chilean Andes rising out of the clouds like monolithic, silent witnesses to the horrors of Torture Island.

From what he could see, Chant judged the island to be quite small—perhaps no more than two or three miles in diameter, with all of the facilities rather tightly packed together in this particular area. The concrete square where the sidewalks met served, to judge from the grease stains Chant had seen on its surface, as a helicopter landing pad. Two or three hundred yards beyond the pad was a complex of buildings—a one-story, windowless building of gleaming white tile with an adjacent cottage, a three-story wood-frame building that looked like a college dormitory, a hut next to a huge radio antenna, and a rather large, dome structure that Chant guessed might be a desalinization plant. Next to the dome structure was a huge bank of solar panels as big as a football field. Except for the cleared area, the rest of the island appeared to be dense brush and small, hardy, wind-twisted trees.

"The shark lagoon is coming right up, Sinclair," Bernard said, raising his voice slightly in order to be heard above the whistling wind. "It's where you're going to end up sooner or later. This little visit will give you something to think about."

They were still within sight of the main complex of buildings when Chant suddenly found himself pushed to the very rim of a commalike formation that had been cut into the body of the island by the action of the sea. In this cavity, the water below was almost mirror-still, protected by a virtual sea wall of towering rock formations at its mouth. There were five shacks, padlocked, farther along the rim of the comma. Near the shacks, jutting out over the lagoon, an ominous-looking scaffold had been constructed. On the scaffolding was a wooden tower and a motorized winch; at the end of the winch rope was attached a large, steel hook.

In the clear deep blue depths of the lagoon, huge, dark shapes glided like shadows of death across the bottom.

"There are two things that end up in this lagoon in large numbers," Bernard continued. "One is sharks, and the other is pearl-bearing oysters. The oysters get torn up from beds during storms and they get washed in; you find a lot of them at the mouths of those underwater caves." Bernard paused, came around to face Chant and smiled thinly. "The sharks come because we feed them."

Chant said nothing. He continued to stare down at the dark shapes in the water while he sought to relax, build up new reserves of energy, and block off the residual pain left by the mute woman who had visited him during the night. He was no longer interested in what Bernard Krowl had to say, and he began to close off his mind to the other man. He was now concerned with Richard Krowl—and what surprises the man with the long, yellow hair and pale eyes might have waiting for him.

"Now I'll show you what guts is all about, Sinclair," Bernard said. *"Yo!"*

At Bernard's shout, one of the broken people who served as servants on the island came limping around from behind the row of shacks. The man, rail-thin and with his right arm hanging at a grotesque angle, came up to Bernard and, without speaking, handed the man a set of keys before turning and hurrying off toward the main complex.

Bernard opened the shack on the far right, went in, then reappeared a few moments later with an armful of diving gear—black rubber wet suit, goggles, snorkel, flippers, knife, and a mesh net. He set everything down except the knife, then opened the door to another shack and went in. There was a scream, the sounds of a brief struggle, and then Bernard emerged dragging an emaciated-looking man who was covered with bruises, cuts, and what appeared to Chant to be burn marks.

Now there were shouts of protest, screams, and loud banging on the doors coming from the other shacks. Haunted, horrified eyes gazed out through slits in the doors.

Bernard's captive began to scream even louder as Bernard proceeded to drag him up on the scaffold, and he struggled with new strength born of desperation. Bernard slapped him hard across the mouth, then hit him in the belly, doubling him over. Then Bernard dragged the man the rest of the way up on the scaffold, threw him down next to the winch tower and proceeded to bind the man's hands.

"Hold it, Bernard!" Chant shouted into the wind. "Don't use that man to impress me! I'm already impressed! Stop it!"

Bernard ignored him. When he had finished tying the man's hands, Bernard effortlessly lifted him up in the air and hung his bound wrists over the hook. Next, Bernard drew his knife from its sheath and slashed the dangling man behind both knees. Blood gushed from the wounds, and the man screamed again as Bernard pushed him off the platform to be left dangling in the air, staring in horror at the black shapes massing below him in response to the blood dripping from his legs. One shark actually lifted its head from the water and gnashed its teeth. The water was starting to roil as dozens of black fins cut the surface of the water, converging on the scent of blood.

Bernard pressed a button on the winch motor. A gasoline-powered engine roared to life. Bernard turned a lever, and the rope with the bleeding man on the end of it began to descend toward the water.

Chant continued to shout at Bernard, but the big American did not even look in his direction as he quickly donned the wet suit and, carrying the rest of his gear, nimbly made his way down a narrow trail that had been cut into the face of the escarpment. Less than a minute later Bernard was standing on a rock shelf at the water's edge, donning his flippers and face mask.

The winch had automatically stopped about four feet above the surface of the water, and the man was now desperately trying to hold his bleeding legs up out of the foaming water as sharks flashed by beneath him. Black heads emerged, maws gaped open, multiple rows of razor-sharp teeth flashed.

With the sharks thus occupied, Bernard slipped silently into the water and immediately disappeared from sight. A few seconds later, Chant saw Bernard's shape emerge from beneath a rock shelf and glide powerfully along the bottom, near the mouths of several underwater caves. His hands moved quickly as he gathered objects off the bottom and dropped them in the mesh net he dragged from a strap slung around his neck.

A black shape darted out from the dark mouth of an underwater cave, circled once around the man, then flashed off toward the maelstrom at the opposite end of the lagoon.

Chant shifted his gaze in time to see a huge head emerge

from the water. Teeth flashed, and the hanging man's right leg disappeared below the knee. Then the sharks were all over him. Blood spurted as the sharks leaped from the water and tore chunks of flesh off the man and each other. In less than fifteen seconds there was nothing left on the hook but two arms, still tied at the wrists, severed just below the elbows.

Almost directly below Chant, Bernard pulled himself back up on the rock shelf just ahead of three dark torpedo shapes that were ambling lazily around the edge of the lagoon in his direction. The big man didn't even glance in the direction of the bloody, disembodied arms as he kicked off his flippers, tossed aside his face mask and immediately began to shuck the oysters with his knife, examining the inside of each and then casting the shells over his shoulder into the clear water.

Chant's iron-colored eyes were cold, and his mouth was set in a thin, firm line as he watched the other man shuck oysters, cast aside the shells. Chant's face gave no indication of the rage building inside him. Patreaux might believe there was something to be gained from studying these people, Chant thought, but he did not. Chant wanted only to break and cut them as they had broken and torn his friend, to torture and kill them as they had tortured and killed others.

If that made him no better than his enemies in the eyes even of some men he respected, Chant thought, then so be it. People like those who operated and used Torture Island, like VanderKlaven with his useless drugs, might as well come from another planet as far as Chant was concerned. They were members of a different species of vile creatures, and Chant's only interest was in destroying, not understanding, them.

He wanted Bernard's death to be special, wanted Bernard to pay far more attention to his own agony than he had to that of the man he had used to feed the sharks.

Bernard finished shucking the oysters, began climbing back up the escarpment. He reached the top, walked toward Chant as he appeared to examine something in his right hand.

"All that trouble for one little puny white sucker," Bernard said with obvious disgust as he stopped in front of the wheelchair.

"What did he do?"

Bernard looked up, blinked. "Who?"

Chant spat, then nodded toward the lagoon. "The man who belonged to those arms."

"Oh, him," Bernard said, casually glancing over his shoulder. "He was political. It seems he and a few others were plotting to overthrow the general who runs his country—at least that's what the general thought. It turned out not to be true, but that didn't make any difference to the general. The general wanted him dead, so he's dead. It was in the contract."

"You going to leave the arms hanging there?"

"Sure," Bernard said with a shrug. "At least for a time. It'll give those other fucks in the shacks something pretty to look at until I need one after the next storm; they've all been contracted for execution after interrogation, and my brother has finished with them." Bernard paused, studying Chant. "What do they want Richard to find out from you, Sinclair?"

"Don't you know?"

"If I knew, I wouldn't be asking you. You're just a fucking crook. Somebody want to know where you keep all your money?"

"It beats me, Bernard—if you'll pardon the pun. I think it's a case of mistaken identity."

"You're not going to have any identity when we get through with you."

"Actually, you may already have gone too far. After that session with Feather, I can't even remember what it is I'm supposed to remember."

"We'll jog your memory."

"Your brother doesn't tell you too much, does he, flunky?"

"Fuck you, Sinclair. Usually, I'm not interested. My brother seems to think you're something special, and that you may need special handling."

Chant smiled thinly. "More special than you give the others? I can't wait to find out what he has in mind."

"Wouldn't Richard be surprised if I wheeled you in over there and you'd already told *me* what it is he's so hot to know?"

"We'd both be surprised. What do you have in mind, Bernard? You going to dangle me down there and let the sharks nibble at my toes until I talk?"

"That sounds like it might be a good idea. What do you think, Sinclair? Would you like to keep those bloody arms company for a while?"

"You're starting to bore me, Bernard. That isn't going to happen."

"No?!" Bernard snapped. "What the hell makes you so sure?!"

"Two reasons. You won't shit unless your brother tells you to, and you're probably already a little worried about the fact that you didn't come when he called. The second reason is that you'd have to take me out of this wheelchair to put me on that hook; you do that, and it'll take me about five seconds to kill you."

Bernard flushed, and for a moment Chant thought he was going to hit him. Then Bernard's gaze abruptly shifted to a point just above and behind Chant's head. Chant looked over his shoulder to find two brown-uniformed guards, Asiatics, flanking him as they gazed with impassive faces at Bernard.

"All right, all right, I'm bringing him," Bernard mumbled, quickly stepping around behind the wheelchair and gripping the handlebars. "Richard should learn to hold his fucking water."

THIRTEEN

Chant was wheeled up the fairly steep grade leading from the shark lagoon to the complex of buildings. By the time they reached and crossed the helicopter pad, Bernard was breathing heavily from the exertion of pushing the wheelchair. The two Asiatics, silent and impassive, walked on either side of the chair.

He was wheeled to the white-tiled, windowless building, which had a wheelchair ramp and swinging doors like the cellblock. Inside the building, Chant glanced to his left and right as he was pushed down a long corridor. There were offices and storerooms off the corridor, as well as a large room filled with computer banks. At the end of the corridor, Chant was wheeled into an office that was spacious and well appointed, but dimly lit. He was stopped in a bright pool of light cast by an overhead spotlight, in front of a huge oak desk.

Dr. Richard Krowl sat behind the desk, and it looked to Chant as if the torture doctor had been up all night. In the tightly focused beam of light cast by his desk lamp, Krowl's long hair gleamed greasily, and there was a stubble of beard on his chin and upper lip. In front of him was a thick dossier that Chant felt certain was his, provided to Krowl by the CIA. When Krowl finally looked up, Chant could see that his pale eyes were red-rimmed.

"I called for you over an hour ago," Krowl said curtly to his brother, standing just behind Chant.

"I guess my beeper wasn't working," Bernard replied in a sullen voice.

"You've been to the shark lagoon."

Bernard came around from behind Chant and took a few steps into the darkness to the right of Krowl's desk. There was a soft clicking sound, and then Bernard came back out into the light. "I wanted Sinclair to see what's waiting for him. I put Gonziaga in."

Color seeped up into Richard Krowl's pale cheeks, and a muscle in his jaw twitched. "Who told you to do that?"

"Hey, look here—!"

"Get out, Bernard. Get dried off and dressed, then come back."

"Don't you want the tray set up?" Bernard's tone was petulant, like a reproved child's.

"Yes," Richard Krowl answered after a short pause. "Let me know when you're prepared."

Chant heard Bernard turn around and walk away down the long corridor. At a nod from Krowl, one of the brown-uniformed guards came around, bent down, and removed two steel clips from what Chant assumed were the battery terminals. The other guard pulled two wires from a retracting receptacle on the wall next to Krowl's desk, plugged them into jacks in the left armrest of the wheelchair.

"What am I plugged into this time?" Chant asked casually.

Richard Krowl pressed a switch to the right of his desk and the office was suddenly flooded with soft, white fluorescent light. Chant was surprised to see the woman called Feather seated on a small divan just behind the desk. She wore faded jeans, tennis sneakers, and a light sweater. Her raven-black hair shimmered as it fell in waves down across her cheeks and over her shoulders. As when Chant had seen her earlier, her eyes were staring straight ahead and were slightly out of focus. The expression on her face was vacant. She sat with her back straight, feet flat on the floor, hands folded almost demurely in her lap.

To the right of the divan, along the wall, were four earthenware pots. Three were filled almost to overflowing with white pearls. The pearls in the fourth, smallest pot gleamed in the light like liquid black fire.

"As a matter of fact, you're plugged into a number of things," Krowl answered at last as one of the guards zipped open the front of Chant's coveralls and taped electrodes to his chest. "How did you get out of Southeast Asia after you deserted?"

"I walked out."

"You won't even tell me that?"

"I just did." Chant nodded toward the pearl-filled pots. "Nice collection you've got there. It must be worth a few million."

"Tell Bernard. I'm sure he'll be interested in your estimate; I'm not. Who helped you get back to the United States?"

"Nobody. So you're just into pain, not money. Saint Bernard is into both. He showed me how he uses other people's guts to collect those things. The man's a real moron, as I'm sure you're aware. I also think I detected just a touch of sibling rivalry. Does having to take care of your moron brother ever try your patience, Krowl?"

"Everyone assumed you were dead. For almost four years they assumed you were dead."

"Did they?"

"Not only did you manage to kill the five men tracking you, every one of them a skilled assassin, but you then managed to move undetected through more than five hundred miles of enemy-held territory—and you did this with everyone hunting you."

"How about that?"

Krowl tapped the papers on his desk. "There's a great deal of information here, but I suspect there's also a great deal missing."

"File a complaint with the people who gave you the dossier."

"I don't believe they know. You've always been a most secretive man, even before you began your new career as international criminal."

"It says that in the dossier?"

"I believe it. As a matter of fact, the CIA has been most forthcoming, but I'm interested in more than an official history of John Sinclair's deeds and misdeeds. It's your personal background that intrigues me."

"Mmmm."

"You're a very impressive man."

"Oh, I'll bet you say that to all the people you torture."

"You always work alone."

"Well, you know how tough it is to find good help these days."

"How is it that Interpol was able to capture you so easily?"

"Easily? They've been after me for almost twenty years."

"Why did you give up without a fight?"

"I didn't feel like getting shot. If I'd known what was being planned for me, I think I'd have chosen the bullets."

"The word *ninja* keeps popping up in written and oral descriptions of you. Did you know a man by the name of Harry Gray?"

"Can't say that I did—or do."

"Are you a *ninja?*"

"What's a *ninja?*"

"Harry Gray fought in Vietnam. The two of you apparently had identical tours of duty."

"So did a few hundred thousand other men."

"Gerard Patreaux?"

"Is that a question?"

"Do you know him?"

"No."

"You were born in Japan, of American parents."

"That's right. I remember."

"Your father was a high-level diplomat who died of a heart attack some years ago. Your mother died a year and a half later. You're a highly educated man, with degrees from both American and European universities—including the Sorbonne. After graduation, you returned to the United States. You enlisted in the Army and specifically requested that you be sent to Vietnam. Why?"

"Why not? I'd never been there."

"At the age of twenty-four, in Officer Candidate School, you defeated the Army's best martial arts instructor; prior to that time, it seems nobody in the Army had even been aware that you had such talent—they certainly didn't teach you. You were offered that man's position, and you turned it down. You could have spent the entire war in the United States, teaching recruits. Yet you chose combat—*insisted* on it. Why?"

"I'd have made a lousy teacher," Chant replied easily, then looked at the woman. "Hello, sweetheart. That was some time you gave me last night."

"You are reputed to be an awesome martial arts expert —perhaps the finest in the world, with proficiency in a wide variety of weapons."

"I should hire you as my press agent, Krowl."

"I asked you if you are a *ninja*."

"I asked you what a *ninja* is."

"In addition to your warrior's skills, you have astounding control over your mind and emotions; *that* I've seen— and am seeing—for myself. I've begun to suspect that you may even be able to exert some considerable control over your autonomic nervous system. You really caught me by surprise yesterday when I examined you in your cell. I wouldn't have thought it possible that any man could have been in your physical and psychological stress-state and still exhibit heartbeat and respiration that fell within a normal range. You had to be afraid."

"Of course I was afraid, Krowl," Chant said simply. "I'm afraid now."

"I know. But you mask it better than any human being I've ever met."

"It's not a question of masking anything; it has to do with not wasting energy."

Krowl studied Chant for some time before he spoke again. His voice was very soft, almost a whisper. "It was quite a feat for you to manipulate all of the men in that room."

"Is that what I did?"

"It's what you tried to do, and you almost succeeded. Even crucified on a stone wall and not knowing what I was going to do to you next, you were absolutely cool—and scheming."

Chant laughed. "Considering the fact that it wasn't your

ass hanging on the wall, you seem to know a lot about what was going on in my mind."

"I merely observed—and marveled. Indeed, I suspect you are trying to manipulate this situation."

"Yeah? How am I doing?"

"I'm not a fool, Sinclair. Surely, you must realize that. And I'm not like these other men. If you had fallen into the hands of any of them, you'd be dead by now—and your secrets would be safe. They would have totally botched the job. I won't."

"Are you looking for my approval, Krowl?" Chant said, and laughed. "You're no fool, but you're the biggest fucking hypocrite *I've* ever met—and I've met a few, believe me. You want to set yourself apart from the other gorillas you have wandering around this place, but it won't play. You're just another gorilla with good grammar, Krowl, a garden-variety torturer with a medical degree and a few kinks. What are you trying to do, bullshit me to death?"

Again, Richard Krowl was silent for some time as he studied Chant, his pale eyes occasionally dropping to the pages of the dossier on the desk in front of him. Finally he looked up and nodded to the two guards, who turned and left.

"Perhaps you're right," Krowl said at last. "Maybe I have been looking to you for . . . something. I'm not sure what. You're a most impressive man, from a personal as well as a medical viewpoint. I don't often get to talk to men of your stature."

"You poor, sad, pretentious son of a bitch. What are you, lonely for refined company? Just because a butcher kills slowly, with precision and without passion, doesn't make him less of a butcher."

"I'm not responsible for your being here, Sinclair. It's your government's responsibility."

"Wrong. It's not even the CIA's responsibility. Let's just

say that I have a few very powerful enemies in very high positions of power, and they feel their interests are jeopardized by things I know. *They're* responsible for my being here, and now *you're* responsible for my suffering, as well as the suffering of every victim who's ever been sent to this place. *You* will be personally responsible for my death. *You* may not take all this personally, Krowl, but I certainly do. You seem to be playing this mind game with yourself where you wind up thinking of yourself as some kind of government contractor providing screwdrivers to the Air Force. That isn't quite the case, Krowl. You hurt and kill people, *Doctor.* You have a cretin brother who feeds live victims to sharks, remember? I'm here to tell you that you operate a chamber of horrors. What the fuck is it *you* think you're doing?"

Krowl seemed disturbed. He ran his fingers through his hair, then turned in his chair and looked at Feather. The woman gave no indication that she knew, or cared, he was studying her, and after a few moments the torture doctor turned back to Chant.

"You've seen the maimed people on this island, Sinclair. I didn't do those things. Those people wouldn't be alive if it weren't for me."

"The shark lagoon, Krowl."

"The man Bernard killed was contracted to die. If he hadn't been killed here, he would have been killed someplace else, by the people who sent him here in the first place. What's the difference?"

Again, Chant laughed. "Krowl, you're a moral and philosophical giant."

"Every subject—"

"Subject?"

"Every man or woman who comes here has been marked for torture and death. In many cases, I make things easier for them. Their fate was sealed before my services were ever contracted for, and their suffering—like yours—is carefully calibrated to resistance."

Chant glanced at the woman, who was still staring vacantly off into space. "There's not a wasted scream around here, right?"

"Right."

"You're just a garbage man who does other people's dirty work for them, Krowl. You also seem to conveniently forget that these people have good reasons not to talk. People you force them to name also end up being killed and tortured. The people whose dirty work you do torture for political or military reasons. You do it for money. You find that a more attractive motive?"

"I care nothing for money, Sinclair!" Richard Krowl snapped. He abruptly rose from his chair, turned, and stepped back toward the divan. He hooked the toe of his shoe over the lip of one of the larger earthenware pots, tipping it over. A thousand white pearls rolled out on the hardwood floor, skittering and clattering around the office, out the door, and down the long corridor. The woman didn't even blink.

"Bernard's going to be upset," Chant said casually as the pearls continued to roll about with a cascading rush of clicks and pops.

"This facility and the services I provide do not increase the amount of suffering in the world by one iota," Krowl said as he eased himself back down into his chair. His face was still flushed, and his pale green eyes seemed unnaturally bright. "The people who are sent here have already been marked. Here, at least, their suffering serves a purpose."

"What purpose?"

The man with the long yellow hair again rose from his chair and walked across the room to a file cabinet. He slid open the top drawer, reached in, and took out a thick folder and a reel of computer tape. "I'm a scientist, Sinclair," Krowl snapped, throwing the folder and the computer tape on the desk. "I'm a research neurologist. The work I do is important! It has value—inestimable value! It is research that involves the complex interface between the mind and the human nervous system. One day this work will be published, and then all the people who've condemned and ridiculed me will be forced to consult my work in order to do their own. The data that's coming out of this research will one day be considered a standard of reference. Do you really think I'd choose to live on this godforsaken island listening to men scream if there were any other way to do this research?!"

Chant did not reply. Again, his gaze shifted back to the woman, and it seemed to him that her eyes grew slightly more focused as Krowl spoke. Chant saw her swallow; the tip of her tongue darted out and licked her lips.

"Pain—or, more precisely, the perception of pain—is a highly individualistic matter," Krowl continued. "You, for example, exhibit an extremely high tolerance for pain. This isn't because your nerves are any less sensitive than the average man's, but because you react to the sensation of what we call 'pain' differently. Things like nervous overload, plateaus of pain, tolerance, the question of why some men and women perceive pain as pleasure—all of these things are poorly understood, and it is my field of research."

"You were born out of your time, Krowl, as well as your place. There were any number of Nazi doctors who used the same rationale for the experiments they conducted on men, women, and children."

"I'm not a Nazi, Sinclair! I don't select the people who are sent here!"

"The German doctors didn't select their victims either, Krowl. And now I understand why they threw you out of medical school. Christ, what kinds of experiments were you trying to do there?"

"There are certain experiments that can only be conducted on humans, because humans are the only species that displays such a wide differential in perception of, and reaction to, pain. It is a legitimate field of study, and one day the work I'm doing here will serve to *alleviate* suffering. Yours is the kind of knee-jerk reaction men who do controversial research have had to contend with down through the centuries."

Chant shook his head, nodded toward Feather. "Why is she here? What did you do to her?"

"Feather has joined us because she is my assistant."

Chant laughed. "Some assistant."

"My research assistant, Sinclair," Krowl said, narrowing his eyes. "Her real name is Maria Gonzalez. It may interest you to know that she's also a physician."

Chant nodded. "It does interest me. I asked what you did to her."

"I didn't do anything to her, except—"

Suddenly the woman called Feather shifted on the couch and shook her head violently. Krowl glanced at her, then looked back at Chant.

"So," Krowl continued quietly, "I think we've chatted long enough, and now it's time to get down to business."

"Don't rush things on my account, Krowl."

Krowl closed Chant's dossier and sighed. "As I've said, you are an exceptional man. A challenge. Perhaps, like others who've been sent to me, you believe that you will die before you reveal to me what it is I want to know—which is to say, what the men who sent you here want to know. I can assure you, Mr. Sinclair, that you will *not* die on me. Among other things, the electrodes attached to your body measure your heartbeat and respiration. Your suffering, as I've indicated, will be calibrated to your resistance.

Beginning today, I'm afraid the procedures used on you will be a bit cruder than what you've experienced so far."

"I thought the other procedures were pretty crude."

"Not as crude as what you'll undergo now. You will tell me what I want to know."

"Will I?"

"Yes. What's more, I think you understand that. Up to now, you might say that I've been trying to get your attention so that we could save time in the long run. Now you know that I'm very good at what I do, Mr. Sinclair. I can bring you to the point of death through horrible suffering, but then I will bring you back again for more horrible suffering. That will continue until you surrender your secrets to me. There is no escape for you, not in life, and not in death. I sincerely would not like to see you become one of the living dead here, like the man who ate your flesh, but that's really up to you. I will—"

"I'm ready." It was Bernard's voice on the intercom speaker just above Chant's head.

Krowl pressed a button beneath his desk, and the wall to Chant's left slid open on recessed tracks to reveal another, larger chamber, which was equipped like an operating room. Very bright lights shone from overhead and were reflected with almost painful brilliance from banks of mirrors set up around the room. There was an operating table with bloodstained leather restraining straps. The floor was constructed of gleaming white tile, with half a dozen drains circling the table. Next to the table was a tray covered with stainless steel surgical instruments that gleamed in the bright lights. Just to the right of the table, built into the wall below a bank of mirrors, was an array of electronic monitors.

Bernard was waiting in the center of the room, a smile on his face. He was standing behind a long, low cart that had two compartments separated by an insulated partition.

One compartment was overflowing with cracked ice, which was melting under the lights, running down the sides of the cart and into the drains set into the floor. In the second compartment was a large socket into which was plugged an electric branding iron.

"So?" Chant said to Richard Krowl as the torture doctor wheeled him into the second room. "What is it you want to know?"

Krowl stopped the wheelchair midway between the operating table and Bernard's cart. When he stepped around and looked down at Chant, there was the faintest glint of surprise in his eyes. "You want to tell me about Operation Cooked Goose?"

"Right."

"Are there documents?"

"Of course. There are three copies of—"

"Just a minute," Krowl said, abruptly holding up his hand. "I want you to think very carefully before you speak."

Chant grunted. "What kind of a torturer are you? I'm ready to tell you what you want to know, but you don't seem to want to hear it."

Krowl studied Chant for some time before he spoke. "It's true that you're exhausted—far beyond what you're willing to show. You're in pain, hungry, thirsty, and undoubtedly afraid. Why, then, do I doubt your willingness to cooperate?"

"That's your problem, Krowl. I hope I don't have to be put through any more because of it. What do you expect me to do?"

"I don't want to hear lies."

"Now, would I lie to you?"

"You won't find things so amusing if you do lie, Sinclair. There are penalties for lying to me when an official interrogation takes place. This will be an official interrogation. The penalties are severe enough to cause considerable physical damage. It's important for you to understand that. Every breath you take is under my control. I may choose to give you time, but there is no way that you can stall for it yourself."

"All right," Chant said evenly.

"Why?"

"Why what?"

"Why are you giving up with no more resistance?"

"Because there's no longer a point to resistance. I can't win. I know a bit about torture myself, Krowl—and you're good. Eventually, you will break me down. I've had time to look around the place and size up your operation. Frankly, if I thought there was any hope of escaping, I'd try to hold out. I no longer have that hope. I assume that your contract calls for my eventual termination?"

"It does . . . of course. You'd know I was lying if I tried to deny it. But then, the notion of death in itself doesn't bother you that much."

"Precisely. I'm not afraid of dying, and I'm willing to endure a good deal of discomfort if I think there's a point. With no hope of successful resistance, there's no point—and no reason for me to go through any more shit. About the only thing I can hope for is to die with my mind intact, and that's what I'd like."

"If you tell the truth, you'll have that."

"Are my reasons good enough for you? It's hard for me to crawl around strapped into this wheelchair, but I can work up a snivel or two if it will make you feel better."

Krowl almost smiled. "A snivel won't be necessary. Yours is the rational reasoning of a rational man—maybe."

"What do you want to know?"

"A great many things, Mr. Sinclair. Frankly, the CIA has their set of interests, and I have mine. I'm hoping you'll be able to satisfy both."

"I'll certainly try."

"I do hope you will. You'll remember what I said about severe penalties for lying?"

Chant glanced down at the wires stretching from his wheelchair back into Krowl's office, then nodded toward the monitors on the wall. "I'll remember," he said. "I assume I'm hooked up to a polygraph or a voice-stress analyzer, maybe both?"

"Both—and more."

"Sure," Chant said with a wry smile. "After all, this is a class operation, right? How am I doing on the machines?"

Krowl said nothing. He stared hard at Chant for a few moments, then abruptly hoisted himself up on the edge of the operating table and casually crossed one leg over the other. Feather glided silently into the room, sat down cross-legged on the floor in front of Chant. She cocked her head sideways and stared up into Chant's face with her empty eyes and vacant expression.

For reasons that he did not understand, the woman's presence made Chant more anxious than the monitors, operating table, surgical instruments, or branding iron. Although he did not know why, he sensed that Feather was the most dangerous instrument in the room, and posed the greatest threat to him.

Bernard tossed a handful of ice into Chant's lap. "Damn, I hope you lie, Sinclair. I'd love to fry your fucking ears off."

"Subject two hundred forty three," Krowl intoned. "Interrogation and termination contract, Central Intelligence Agency." He paused, nodded to Chant. "What is your name?"

"John Sinclair."

"Middle name?"

"No middle name."

"Why are you called 'Chant'?"

"You'll laugh—and you won't believe me."

There was a hollow click as Bernard removed the electric branding iron from its socket. The six-inch heating element at the tip glowed white hot as Bernard stepped up to the wheelchair and brought the glowing metal close to Chant's left cheek, just below his eye. Chant could smell his hair singeing.

"Indulge me," Richard Krowl said dryly.

"It was a nickname I picked up in boot camp, and it just stuck."

"How did you get the nickname?"

"I used to sing in the shower. I don't have much of a singing voice."

Richard Krowl leaned back and consulted something on the other side of the table, hidden from Chant's view. Then he glanced up at the monitors.

Chant waited, squinting against the terrible heat of the branding iron, smelling his hair burn.

The torture doctor, apparently satisfied, straightened up, nodded with his head for Bernard to move away. The heat dissipated, and Bernard uttered a disappointed grunt.

"Where were you born?"

"Osaka, Japan."

"Age?"

"Forty-four. Incidentally, you were right on about my being hungry and thirsty. Is there any reason why I can't have a snack while we're about this?"

"What branch of the service were you in?"

"United States Army Special Forces."

"Were you a double agent?"

"Not unless you count serving as a soldier and a CIA operative at the same time as being a double agent. We often felt that way."

"You never worked for the Russians?"

"Not for the Russians, and not for any other foreign power."

"Were you ever approached?"

"All the time. Everybody knew everybody else."

At a motion from Richard Krowl, the branding iron came close to his cheek again.

"Are you sure?"

"I'm sure."

The heat went away.

The questioning continued for hours, with many of the same questions repeated over and over again: Chant's childhood, his education, his training in the martial arts, his desertion, Operation Cooked Goose, the documents he held and the arrangements he had made for their dissemination, people he had talked to, his activities in the years since he had deserted, his residences.

Chant answered the questions in a flat monotone while Bernard paced behind him, branding iron in hand, disappointment and increasing anger smouldering in his eyes and twisting his thuggish face out of shape. Occasionally he would look hopefully to his brother, but Richard Krowl ignored him.

At one point food and water were brought by the broken man and woman who had first attended Chant in his cell. The cuffs on Chant's wrists were released, and he was allowed to eat and drink while the questioning went on, hour after hour. Occasionally, Richard Krowl would refer to Chant's dossier, which he kept open beside him on the operating table, and then repeat a question he might have asked a dozen times before.

Krowl showed no signs of tiring—nor did Feather. Through the endless hours of interrogation, the woman had not moved, not even to go to the toilet or even change her position. She had not eaten or drunk anything; she simply sat cross-legged on the floor, staring vacantly up into Chant's face.

After yet another series of questions on Operation Cooked Goose and the documents Chant held in his possession, it finally seemed to be over. Krowl sighed deeply, stretched, then got off the table and began to idly examine a few areas on the yards of paper tape that had spewed out over the tile floor from the polygraph machine behind the table. He pushed the pile of paper aside with his foot, then took a cigar out of an inside pocket and lit it with a gold butane lighter.

"Some tough nut you are, Sinclair," Bernard whispered hoarsely in Chant's ear. "In the end it turns out that you're nothing but one big fucking pussycat."

Krowl blew a large, blue smoke ring, waved it away with his hand, then turned around and looked inquiringly at Feather.

Feather looked up at Krowl and very slowly shook her head. Then she rose and walked quickly from the room.

Chant watched the woman go, and felt the muscles in his stomach begin to tighten. Suddenly he felt cold, and there was a tingling sensation along the base of his spine. He turned back to find Krowl staring at him.

The torture doctor clamped the cigar between his teeth, abruptly reached out to the side of the operating table and flicked a switch. The lights in the operating room dimmed at the same time as lights behind one of the banks of mirrors came up, revealing a viewing gallery in which sat the dozen torturers who were Krowl's guests on the island. All of the men appeared exhausted—yet also strangely exhilarated, and most impressed. Cigar and cigarette smoke made the air in the gallery look blue, and the aisles between the two steeply banked areas of seats were littered with paper and plastic food and drink containers. Krowl flicked another switch, activating a two-way public address system; the men in the gallery could be heard talking excitedly to one another.

"Gentlemen," Krowl said around his cigar.

"Bravo!" someone in the gallery shouted.

Krowl squinted into the lights as he studied the faces above him. "So," he said, removing the cigar from his mouth. A few of the men began to clap, and Krowl motioned impatiently for them to stop. "In slightly less than three days I have extracted information from a man all of you predicted would die before he'd give me the time of day. Indeed, as you noticed, there was no resistance at all once we had begun. You've been privy to everything that has been done to this man, and now I'd like to hear your thoughts."

There appeared to be an initial reluctance to speak, but finally a few of the men began to offer their opinions and observations. All expressed their admiration for Krowl's patience, his coolness, and his skilfull application of both pain and pleasure. Even Chester Norham, who had apparently been returned to the good graces of Krowl and the others, had something to say—although he avoided looking at Chant.

Chant, increasingly uneasy, found himself constantly turning his head and glancing toward Krowl's office, where Feather had gone.

When the men had finished speaking, Krowl laughed without humor, reached out and touched the glowing tip of his cigar to the middle of one of the folds of polygraph readout paper. A dark smudge with a cherry-red center appeared on the paper and began to spread.

"It's all very neat," Richard Krowl said. He glanced up

at the torturers, then at Bernard, who was watching his brother with a mystified expression on his face. "The problem is that the information Mr. Sinclair has so graciously provided us with is a carefully constructed tissue of lies."

Chant began preparing himself; hopelessness, desperation, frustration, terror, panic—all had to be brushed aside, vanquished, as he stilled himself in order to marshal the inner forces he needed to trigger the ultimate weapon he carried within his mind.

He had been defeated by the most dangerous instrument in the room, Chant thought, the most sensitive lie detector —Feather. Krowl was ignoring the reams of polygraph and voice-stress analyzer readouts that indicated he was telling the truth, relying instead on a simple shake of the head offered by the strange, mute woman torturer.

Of course, Chant thought, Krowl was absolutely correct in doing so.

"Lies," Richard Krowl continued as he burned more holes in the paper. "There is, of course, some truth here; questions concerning facts that could be verified by checking his dossier or other sources were answered truthfully. Perhaps some of the other questions were answered truthfully, perhaps not. The point is that we don't know. Certainly, John Sinclair has lied about every single *important* thing that we wanted to know."

There were murmurs of astonishment and disbelief from the men in the viewing gallery. Suddenly a strip of paper burst into flame and quickly spread. Krowl kicked the burning paper aside, then turned his back on the flames.

Acrid smoke swirled in Chant's face as he continued his preparations for the supreme exercise in body control he was certain he would need within moments, when Bernard would be ordered to come at him with the branding iron.

"There are only two groups of individuals who could defeat this type of lie detector equipment," Krowl continued in an almost conversational tone. "Psychotics could do it, for they themselves are usually unable to distinguish between the fact and fiction in their own minds; their respiration, galvanic skin reaction, and pulse rate may indicate they're telling the truth even when they're telling the most outrageous lies. Of course, that's because the psychotic may believe he's telling the truth.

"The second group is comprised of men like Mr. Sinclair—although he is the best I have ever encountered. He is so good that you may think of him as making up a third group, of which he is the only member. These individuals understand just what it is the machines record—stress, which is normally self-induced in response to the anxiety produced by telling a lie. Quite simply, these men are able to control their reactions. I've met a few who do it by entering into a self-induced, trancelike state. It's something to watch for. However, obviously, to successfully play this kind of game with a hot poker virtually stuck in your ear is a feat of incredible virtuosity."

"How can you be certain he's lying?" the Greek colonel asked.

"I'm certain," Krowl replied brusquely. "The point here is that, in the final analysis, you must rely on your own instincts."

Chant felt Bernard come up behind him, felt the heat of the white-hot branding iron growing on the side of his face. He was ready, his mind still, armed, prepared . . .

In another millisecond, as the iron touched him . . .

"No, Bernard," Richard Krowl said.

"Let me burn him!" Bernard shouted, coughing on the smoke that was rising from the burning papers, filling the room. "Damn it, Richard, you've *gotta* let me burn him now! He's making fools out of us!"

"No, Bernard," the torture doctor repeated simply. "Do as I say, please. Back away."

Almost a minute passed. Then Bernard cursed, and the heat moved away from Chant's face.

Still Chant waited, poised, the weapon in his mind triggered . . .

"You're a magician, John Sinclair," Richard Krowl continued quietly, looking down at Chant as he waved smoke away from his face. "You are, indeed, a *ninja*—as advertised. What the CIA wants to know is insignificant compared to the other secrets of power, self-control, and will you carry in your mind and body. I want to know what those secrets are." He paused, reached out and took the glowing branding iron from Bernard. "Take him back to his cell," he commanded his brother.

"Damn it, Richard—!"

"Be quiet," the torture doctor said, then turned around to look up at the perplexed faces in the viewing gallery. "Gentlemen, I believe you will find the few days you have remaining here of special interest."

Apparently he was not finished yet, Chant thought, and he slowly began to relax both the muscles of his body and the invisible muscles of his mind. As he was wheeled toward the office, he lowered his head slightly, began to take deep, measured breaths.

Without warning, the white-hot branding iron was slapped across his left shoulder. Chant had the sensation of liquid fire flowing across his skin, rushing through his veins as the smell of scorched fabric and burning flesh mingled with that of burning paper in his nostrils. Then Chant screamed and passed out.

FOURTEEN

SLOWLY, AS IF surfacing from the bottom of a very deep well filled with black water, Chant swam up to consciousness, the pain in his left shoulder serving as a kind of lifeline that he climbed sensation by sensation, thought after thought. Finally he opened his eyes, blinked in surprise, slowly and painfully eased himself up into a sitting position and looked around.

He was back in his cell. His wrists and ankles were shackled, but the chains were slack and he was lying on a thin but comfortable mattress with a blanket thrown over him. The temperature in the cell was comfortable. The taste of burnt metal in his mouth indicated to him that he had been drugged to keep him unconscious for an unknown length of time. However, he had been bathed and dressed in clean coveralls, and the burn wound on his shoulder had been dressed and partially anesthetized. Beside the mattress was a large thermos bottle and a tray on which was arrayed a selection of cold meats and bread. When he opened the thermos, the dizzying aroma of rich, black coffee wafted up into his nostrils.

He was being primed again, Chant thought. He had been taken to the edge of an abyss, shown a universe of agony. Now he was being soothed, relaxed, his emotions, flesh, muscles, and nerves given time to recover only so that the torment to come would be felt to its maximum.

The darkness in the corridor outside the cell's peephole told Chant that it was night, which meant that he might reasonably expect a return visit from Feather after he had fed himself and rested. He would, of course, eventually be allowed to pass out, and he would awaken to find himself in the wheelchair. Once again Bernard would wheel him back to the torture chamber inside the windowless building, where once again Richard Krowl would question him, and once again . . .

It was absolutely sound technique, Chant thought, just as Krowl had outlined it to his resident torturers. He was supposed to dwell on the horrors to come, even as he enjoyed the food, coffee, warmth, and rest provided to him. Krowl was a worthy opponent, and the only flaw Chant could see in the torture doctor's plan was that he wouldn't be in the cell when Feather, Bernard, or anyone else came for him.

He had held out long enough to get the information he needed—some idea of the layout of Krowl's Torture Island complex, the number of people here, and the nature of the security. He'd had his guided tour of the facility, and had survived relatively intact, with no permanent damage.

Now it was time to go to work.

There were no television cameras in the cell, and Chant had seen none in the outer corridor. Nor had there been a guard posted outside the cellblock—at least there hadn't been when Bernard had wheeled him out. Still, as a precaution against someone looking in on him, Chant rolled over on his side, facing the wall, before starting to recover the weapons and tools planted on and in his body before he had returned to Amsterdam. He unzipped the front of his coveralls, searched in his thick chest hair with the tips of his fingers until he found a small nub of glue. Gripping the nub of glue between thumb and forefinger, he plucked it off his skin, then proceeded to unravel the two yards of fine, ultrastrong piano wire that had been woven into the hair and spot-glued to the flesh. This done, he wrapped the length of wire loosely around his left wrist and secured it in such a way that it could be whipped off almost instantaneously. He did not need the extra yard of wire woven into his pubic hair, and he left that in place.

Using the hardened fingernail on his right hand, he slit open tiny, flesh-colored sutures in the calluses beneath both big toes. Beneath both of the calluses was a square of steel comprised of jointed, collapsing sections. When pulled apart, each section became a strong but flexible two-inch steel pick, and an interlocking joint at the end of each made it possible to double the length of the pick. Chant used one section to pick open the locks on his wrist and ankle shackles, then joined the sections together and set the larger pick aside.

With his sharp, hardened nails he cut off two strips of the mattress covering, wrapped these around his right wrist.

Next he slit open the callus beneath his left heel and removed what appeared to be pressed seaweed sealed in plastic wrap. In fact, the substance was a mixture of herbs that, when ingested, acted upon the nervous system with speed and power greater than that of the most powerful amphetamine. He chewed slowly on the herb mixture, then washed it down with coffee. Immediately, his head cleared, his exhaustion left him, and his nerves and muscles leapt to life.

There were more items, but Chant saw no need for them at the moment, and he left them in place.

He quickly ate the cold cuts on the tray, drank half of the coffee in the thermos. With the long pick in hand, he rose and went to the heavy wooden door. He put his ear to the peephole and listened, but heard no one moving outside. He dropped to one knee, inserted the pick in the lock, and in less than a minute had opened it. He rose, pulled the door open.

With the powerful stimulant galvanizing his muscles and sharpening his senses, Chant glided, silent as the night that shrouded him, to his left down the corridor, up the wheelchair ramp. He listened for a few moments inside the swinging doors. When he heard nothing, he quickly pushed through the doors, darted to his right, and pressed back against the building. The full moon was partially obscured by scudding clouds. Chant waited and watched, but could detect no movement in the direction of the main complex, nor in the direction of the shark lagoon.

Chant scooped up a handful of loose dirt from the base of the building, rubbed it over his face, his hands, and the tops of his feet. Then, keeping low, he darted away from the building to his left, down the grade leading to the shark lagoon.

The stimulant had erased his fatigue and given him strength, but it also severely magnified the pain from both his bite and burn wounds. Chant used *po-chaki* to isolate the pain, then—free at last and hidden in night—allowed himself to indulge the emotions he'd had to keep so carefully in check from the moment he'd walked out of Hugo VanderKlaven's office in Amsterdam to the waiting Bo Wahlstrom.

What he felt most was an almost overwhelming rage—never experienced more strongly than when, strapped into the wheelchair, he had been forced to mask his emotions, sit and listen to the torture doctor who had crushed, burned, slashed, and twisted the life out of Harry Gray describe himself as a "researcher."

He was going to enjoy giving Richard Krowl his heartfelt reaction.

Somehow, Chant thought, his friend had found a way to get on the island, then off again—after pocketing one of the Krowls' black pearls. How Harry had done that remained a mystery, but it indicated to Chant that, despite Gerard Patreaux's description of the island, there might be a way to navigate a boat in and out through the coral reefs. It was what Chant intended to check out now. He was not concerned about time, his escape being discovered, or of being hunted. The combined forces on the island were not capable of finding, much less capturing, him. Indeed, Chant preferred that Krowl spread out his men to search for him; it would make it easier to pick them off one by one. But it didn't really make any difference to Chant whether they came to him, or he went to them. Krowl would not think to radio for help until it was too late.

Tonight, Torture Island would be *his* killing ground.

Although Chant intended to explore the possibility of escaping the island by sea, he fully expected to leave the way he had originally planned—by air, after he had commandeered the transport helicopter that shuttled men and supplies back and forth from the Chilean mainland. Judging from what Krowl had said to his guests, Chant assumed that he had three—perhaps four—days to wait for the helicopter's scheduled arrival. That was fine with Chant, who was quite willing to wait, enjoying the sun and the sea with the only other people he intended to see survive this night—Krowl's broken people, and any other prisoners he might find. If anyone came earlier to investigate why there was no longer any radio communication with the island, so much the better.

Then it would be back to Switzerland, along a carefully prescribed route already prearranged and being set up by Gerard Patreaux. With Krowl's computer tapes and files in Patreaux's hands, it was most unlikely that any nation or organization named in them would ever finance or use a facility like Torture Island again. Amnesty, Inc. would be allowed to pick up, and care for, the broken people.

It seemed a simple and effective plan, Chant thought as he loped along the edge of the precipice. But no plan was foolproof—which, in his mind, necessitated this search. If there was an opening in the reefs, there was a possibility that Krowl kept a power boat, or even a sailboat for recreation, anchored in a cove.

He passed along the rim of the shark lagoon. Below, shapes moved like black clouds in a liquid sky of midnight blue. Just beyond the comma of the lagoon, the cleared area ended abruptly at a border of waist-high scrub brush and dwarf trees scoured and bent into twisted shapes by the incessant wind. Chant had still sighted nothing at the base of the precipice but jagged reefs and crashing surf, which also guarded the mouth to the shark lagoon.

Chant kept going, stepping carefully through the brush and around the trees, gliding as silently through the dense overgrowth as if he were on open ground. A hundred yards from the border of brush, the terrain became hillier, and he slowed to ease the pressure on his wounds. His belly wound had begun to bleed from his exertions, but not enough to concern him.

He deviated slightly from his path along the edge of the precipice to climb a steep hill, pausing at the crest and looking out over the expanse of the island. From here, he could see to the other side. There was plenty of cover for him to hide in, if necessary, but no sign of any trails—which indicated to him that there was no boat anchored anywhere around the perimeter of the island. He'd seen enough.

He turned to go back, caught a flash of movement out of the corner of his eye. He moved a few yards to his left along the crest of the hill, stood behind a tree and looked down the opposite side of the hill.

Feather was standing, unmoving, on the very edge of the precipice, staring out to sea. The wind was blowing hard where she stood, whipping her raven-black hair back around her face, but she gave no indication that she was cold—or that she even noticed the wind at all. She simply stood still and stared. . . .

His first victim, Chant thought as he glided silently down the hillside. The woman was not armed, and the wind would carry away any scream she might utter, so there was no reason for him to stop a few yards behind her, as he did. He was not sure why he stopped when all he had to do was walk up and push her to her death. It was not her sex; she was part of Krowl's staff on Torture Island, had hurt him more than any man ever had, and had undoubtedly done the same to other men—and perhaps women.

But he remembered Bernard's strange reference to her, as well as Richard Krowl's almost deferential behavior toward her. There was her refusal to let the torture doctor talk about her.

This woman was the human lie detector who had almost cost him his life, Chant thought. Yet she seemed to be so much more. She was, according to Krowl, a physician; yet, like Krowl, she had turned her skills to produce suffering instead of healing. There was no reason for her not to die—unless she too was a victim, as her muteness and strange, vacant expression would seem to indicate. Gerard Patreaux had spoken of the bizarre relationship that often develops between torturer and victim, and it had occurred to Chant while he was sitting in Krowl's office that the torture doctor might love the woman, and she him.

Was Dr. Maria Gonzalez, Feather, more tortured than torturer? Chant was not sure. And if he was not sure, he could not kill her.

Neither, considering the agony she had caused him, was he going to forget about her.

Chant glided forward. Feather seemed to sense his presence at the last moment. She started to turn, but by then Chant was directly behind her, his left arm across her shoulder and his hand over her eyes. With his thumb and middle finger anchored firmly on her temples, he could easily have crushed her skull; instead, he turned her around with his left hand and clipped her across the jaw with his right, knocking her unconscious.

Gerard had wanted a torturer to interview, Chant thought with a wry smile as he made his way back up the hillside, leaving the woman sprawled at the edge of the precipice. Because Feather did not talk didn't mean that she could not. She might well be his gift to the Swiss, along with Krowl's records. He would decide later, perhaps when he had more information on the woman.

She could still die at his hands this night.

In the meantime, he intended to make certain that Feather, when she did regain consciousness, found herself with far fewer companions on Torture Island.

FIFTEEN

CHANT'S FIRST ORDER of business was to secure a sizeable sampling of computer tapes and records, in the event an alarm was raised and he found it difficult to get to them later; he could not risk having them moved, or even destroyed. His initial stop would be the windowless building containing Krowl's office and the torture chamber.

His first victim was a brown-uniformed guard sitting on the grass outside the building, idly smoking a cigarette and staring up at the stars. Chant killed him instantly with a single, bone-shattering blow to the skull, then dragged the body to a drainage ditch beside the building, where he crouched, motionless, for almost a minute. When he saw and heard no one else, he rose and loped around to the front, walked up the wheelchair ramp and through the swinging doors.

Inside the building it was totally dark, but Chant remembered not only the way but the distance to Krowl's office, and he moved quickly and with confidence to it, reached to a wall panel on his left and turned on the lights.

He went first to the metal filing cabinet behind Krowl's oak desk. It was locked, but Chant was able to open it with his pick within moments. From the top drawer he removed three reels of computer tape and set them down on top of the desk, which was bare except for a single manila folder. Out of curiosity, Chant turned on the desk lamp and opened the folder.

The papers inside the folder were written in Russian, with an accompanying English translation. The documents concerned Viktor and Olga Petroff, the Soviet dissidents who had been objects of Amnesty, Inc.'s intense curiosity for months.

Chant scanned the documents in the original Russian, found nothing that was not known, or was not guessed. Three years before, for reasons that remained incomprehensible to the Soviet leaders, the brilliant, internationally famous scientist and his wife had become extremely vocal activists for human rights inside the Soviet Union, incessantly lobbying for Russian adherence to the Helsinki Accords. There had been meetings with Western reporters, written manifestos. The Soviet leaders had not been pleased.

Finally, there had been the banishment to Gorky. Hidden from the eyes of the world, the man and wife had been subjected to labor camps, and even to two months of intensive "psychiatry" in a Russian "mental hospital," in an effort to force them to publicly recant their views and accusations. Nothing had worked, and the Russians were not willing to risk being caught physically harming the two international *cause célèbres*. Now, while the Soviet Union continued to claim that the dissidents were alive and well in Gorky, they were to be sent to Torture Island, where Richard Krowl was to apply his methods to convince the Petroffs of the error of their ways so that they could be safely, publicly, returned to Soviet society, with no further fear of embarrassment; and if they appeared a bit glassy-eyed or absentminded to Western reporters, this was an acceptable risk. They were to be brought to Torture Island at the end of the week.

Good, Chant thought as he closed the folder and pushed it to one side. He would take delivery of the Petroffs when they arrived, and he was certain the man and woman would be happy to accompany him back to Switzerland.

Chant opened a second drawer in the file, began removing files and stacking them on the desk.

The Petroffs.

There could be a problem, Chant thought. Rescuing them might not be so easy; in fact, it might not even be possible. Breaking the collective will of the Petroffs had to be the most sensitive, and potentially explosive, assignment Krowl had ever been given. Certainly, special arrangements were being made all along the line: for the couple's transportation, in absolute secrecy, halfway around the world, as well as for their transfer to Torture Island. The numerous right-wing dictatorships in South America were not exactly friends of the Soviet Union, and it was a measure of the Russians' desperation that they would be willing to deal with Krowl in the first place.

Chant found the switch beneath the desk that opened the wall separating the office from the torture chamber. He flicked the switch, went into the other room and began to look around.

He knew that the transfer of the Petroffs would be accompanied by the strictest security—Russian security. KGB agents would undoubtedly travel with them all the way, no matter what route was taken. There wouldn't be many, for they wouldn't want to attract attention, but they would be top men, very well trained. They would know there could be no slipups, and they would take no chances.

There was nothing in the torture chamber Chant considered worth taking, and he went back into the office, where he began looking for something to carry the materials in.

The Russians might or might not use Krowl's regular shuttle helicopter, but they would certainly conduct a radio check before bringing the Petroffs over from the mainland. Perhaps there were codes. Without doubt, the KGB would insist on radio contact with Krowl. But Krowl would be dead, and the radio would not be operating. . . .

Chant removed the slipcovers from the two cushions on the divan behind Krowl's desk, noting with some amusement as he did so that he had not stepped on a single loose pearl since entering the building. All of the pearls that Krowl had spilled had been carefully collected and returned to one of the larger earthenware pots.

The Petroffs were not going to be delivered. . . .

Chant put the computer tapes and manila folders in one of the slipcovers, poured all of the pearls into the other, zipped up both.

The couple would be returned to Russia—to permanent internal exile, more hospitals and mind-bending drugs, separation, or even execution. The Russians might well write them off, and then simply ignore the rest of the world.

There was nothing that could be done about it now, Chant thought as he picked up the two full slipcovers, went out of the office, and started down the long corridor. He could not undo what he had already done, even if that were a reasonable alternative. Infiltrating the island as a prisoner had been, to say the least, extremely risky, and had been done because it seemed his only option. He had been lucky to survive, and would certainly not have survived another three or four days, assuming he had known the Petroffs were coming and had chosen to wait. It had taken all of his will and courage to subject himself to the hell he'd known he would have to endure. Even if it were possible to go back to his cell before his escape was detected, he did not think he could again achieve the finely tuned psychological state he required for the control he would need. He could not face another three days of torment.

The torment the Petroffs faced would last the rest of their lives. . . .

Chant reached the swinging doors, stopped and stared at them.

He probably would not survive, he thought.

The Petroffs would definitely not survive. . . .

Maybe there wouldn't be special arrangements; maybe the couple would simply be flown in on the shuttle helicopter, which Chant would capture; maybe there were no codes, no radio checks; maybe no helicopter would arrive earlier to investigate the radio blackout; maybe everything would still go according to plan, and he could rescue the Petroffs.

Nonsense, Chant thought, and hissed with frustration.

But the genie was already out of the bottle; he'd attacked Feather, killed a guard.

Feather hadn't seen his face; Krowl wouldn't know it had been him.

But Krowl would report the incidents to the Russians, warn them to stay away.

No. This had to be Krowl's most important assignment, and—perhaps—his greatest opportunity. He would, right up to the last moment, cover up and try to solve the problem himself.

He did not believe he could work up the courage and will to go back.

How had the Petroffs worked up the will and courage to

speak out as they had done, and to persist . . . ?

There were so many imponderables, so many unknowns.

As things now stood, there were no imponderables or unknowns as far as Viktor and Olga Petroff were concerned. Two of the most courageous human beings on the face of the earth would have their minds erased, be destroyed. . . .

He was their only hope.

What would his father have advised?

There would have been no advice. As when he had been offered the ultimate trial of Black Flame, his father would have said only that he must find his own way.

What would his *sensei* say?

They'd say he was out of his fucking mind, Chant thought, and he chuckled softly to himself as he pushed out through the swinging doors into the night.

SIXTEEN

CHANT SNAPPED THE neck of a second guard, who was apparently searching for his companion, and dropped that corpse into the drainage ditch alongside the first. Then he hurried across the cleared area into the brush and trees just beyond the helicopter landing pad. Using a stick, he scooped out two shallow holes in the sandy soil. He put the slipcovers containing the pearls and Krowl's records into the holes, then covered them with soil and brush. When he was finished, there was no sign that the area had been disturbed.

The guns he had taken from the guards were carefully placed in the hearts of two thick, thorny bushes at the very edge of the cleared area, parallel to the helicopter landing pad, fifteen yards apart.

Next he went back to the drainage ditch, hoisted both

dead guards by their belts, then dragged them back the way he had come, taking a route close to the high brush in order not to create a silhouette against the sky. When he reached the edge of the cliff overlooking the shark lagoon, he effortlessly lifted each corpse above his head, tossed it out to fall down toward the dark water and the even darker shapes relentlessly cruising beneath its surface.

What was done couldn't be undone, Chant thought with a grim smile as he once again headed up the slope toward the complex of buildings—and so he might as well do some more. Indeed, the more confusion and terror he created, the better it might be for him; it would give Krowl and the others something to think about other than John Sinclair.

If he was not going to leave Torture Island alive, Chant thought, at least he was going to make sure he had plenty of company on the way to hell.

Chant had not expected to find any more guards awake, and there weren't any. He circled the three-story dormitory building, found two unlocked entrances, and a fire escape at the rear. There were two lights—one in a room on the third floor, and one on the first.

Chant climbed the fire escape, tested a window on the second floor and found it open. He eased the window open, slipped silently into the room.

He found a husky Latin asleep in an adjoining bedroom. Chant took the strips of cloth he had cut from his mattress off his wrist, wrapped them around the palms of both hands. Then he uncoiled the piano wire and wrapped the ends around his hands, leaving a length of about two feet.

"Rise and shine," Chant said, and kicked the foot of the bed.

"Huh-?" The husky man groaned, opened his eyes, then sat bolt upright and started to shout when he saw Chant.

Chant poked his heel in the man's solar plexus, doubling the man over. Then he tore the blanket off the bed to cover his clothes, looped the piano wire around the man's neck and yanked.

The wire cut through the flesh, cartilage and vertebrae of the man's neck like a razor going through cheese. The severed head dropped to the floor, bounced, rolled a few feet, and came to rest on its bloody stump, the eyes still open and the mouth moving as blood from the top of his torso spurted and sprayed over the ceiling, walls, and floor of the bedroom.

Chant tossed the bloody blanket covering him aside, then crossed the hall and dispatched his second torturer in the same manner.

He decided to choose his third victim from a different area. He left the room, went to the end of the corridor, and climbed the stairway there to the third floor. He stalked along the corridor, stopped on impulse when he came to a room with light shining under the door.

The two guards had died instantly, Chant thought, and the two torturers had been barely awake when he'd lopped their heads off. It would give him pleasure to have at least one victim fully conscious, aware of who it was taking his life.

Chant put his ear to the wood of the door and listened, but heard no sound of radio, conversation, or moving about. If the layout of this room was the same as the other two, the door off the corridor opened into a small sitting room, which was adjoined to a bedroom with a door at the far end of the sitting room, on the right. There was a bathroom off the bedroom, and Chant suspected that was where this particular tenant was, if he wasn't reading in bed.

Chant slowly tried the doorknob; it turned. He opened

the door a crack and waited; he still heard no sound. Then he pushed open the door and crouched, ready to spring.

The sitting room was empty.

Chant moved into the room, closing the door silently behind him. Then he moved along the right-hand wall to the open bedroom door, peered through the crack at the jamb. Through this narrow space he could not see the bed, but he did not have to; the light was on in the bathroom, the door was open, and there were now distinct sounds of gastric distress coming from inside.

Chant removed the strips of cloth from his hands, put them back around his wrist. He rewrapped the piano wire around his other wrist, then slipped silently into the bedroom. He stopped, smiling with pleasure when he saw the wooden valet at the foot of the bed. Draped neatly on the valet was a familiar-looking uniform, and at the base of the valet was a pair of black shoes polished to a high gloss.

"Having some problems with the tummy, Colonel?" Chant asked as he stepped into the open doorway of the bathroom.

The pockmarked, swarthy face of the Greek colonel, already pale, went even paler when he looked up from where he was sitting on the toilet and saw the man with the iron-colored eyes and hair standing before him. His mouth dropped open and he started to scream, but Chant pivoted on the ball of his left foot and his right foot swung in an arc through the air, the instep catching the Greek on the side of the head, stifling his scream and knocking him off the toilet seat to the floor.

Instantly, Chant was on the other man. The colonel, his pajama bottoms tangled around his ankles, was desperately trying to scramble to his feet while animal-like moans of terror escaped from his throat. Chant punched him hard in the right kidney, dropping the man to the floor and knocking the wind out of him. Then Chant wrapped his fingers in the man's hair and yanked him up to his knees. He turned the man's face toward the toilet, then used his right hand to violently push the Greek's head into the bowl, down into the foul water. The man struggled desperately, his arms flailing about and his tangled legs scrambling, but Chant easily held him in his firm grip.

Gradually, the man's struggles grew weaker—and then stopped altogether. More waste evacuated from the colonel's bowels, and then the body slumped and went limp. Chant released his grip.

He drew water in the tub, then sat on the edge and carefully washed the blood from his hands and forearms, and the grass stains and dirt from his bare feet. Within ten minutes, he had erased any evidence of his night's work from his body and clothes.

The first rays of dawn were beginning to glow when he climbed out of the room onto the fire escape. There was still no one about, and Chant raced the approach of day back to the cellblock.

He was almost certain that his escape had gone undetected, for otherwise there would surely be guards and torturers running around looking for him. Still, he paused at the top of the ramp, just behind the swinging doors, and listened; there was no sound from inside the building.

Chant pushed through the swinging doors and walked down the long corridor. The door to his cell was ajar, just as he had left it. He had already made his decision, and he did not hesitate now to step into the cell, close the door behind him, and relock it with his pick.

He removed the strips of cloth from his wrist, stuffed them into the mattress. Then he used the piano wire to secure his lock pick to a chain, near the shackle for his right hand, in such a way that the wire and pick would be virtually invisible, except under close inspection. This done, he drank the rest of the coffee in the thermos and ate the remaining cold cuts.

It could be some time, he thought, before he ate and drank again—if ever.

Then he clicked the shackles shut on his wrists and ankles, lay down on the mattress.

And waited.

SEVENTEEN

THEY CAME AN hour later.

A key rattled in the lock, and the door swung open. Bernard and the two remaining guards burst in, stopped, and stared at him. The faces of all three men were ashen, their eyes wide and bright with shock, fear, and disbelief. They seemed at once relieved and disappointed to find him there.

Chant sat up and blinked sleepily. "Good morning, gentlemen."

Bernard cursed, hurried across the cell and perfunctorily rattled Chant's chains and tested the locks on the shackles. Then he nodded to the two other men, and they hurried out of the cell, with Bernard slamming the door shut behind him.

Chant waited another hour. Satisfied that Krowl and his

people were going to be otherwise occupied for some time, he freed himself from the shackles, opened the cell door, and went to the end of the corridor, where he opened the swinging doors a crack and looked out.

Krowl and his people were, indeed, otherwise occupied. The nine remaining torturers, some still in pajamas or bathrobes, had been rousted out of the dormitory and gathered together on the helicopter pad. Richard and Bernard Krowl stood off to one side, machine pistols in their hands. The two guards and a number of broken people appeared to be conducting a search of the dormitory and the adjacent grounds.

Chant smiled grimly, then returned to his cell and locked the door, replaced the manacles on his wrists and ankles.

He could appreciate Richard Krowl's dilemma. Chant now strongly suspected that, except for the prisoners awaiting execution in the shacks by the shark lagoon, he was the only "subject" on the island. The two or three men in the shacks were undoubtedly broken and starved, incapable of the acts that had been perpetrated during the night. And, besides, those men were still locked in the shacks. Having found him still shackled in a locked cell, Richard Krowl would have to conclude that it was one of his guests who was responsible for the three murders, the disappearance of two guards, and a large sampling of his records. Krowl would not be amused; every room, every possession, would be turned inside out in the search for the records and the fortune in pearls.

Eventually, of course, the search would have to turn to the surrounding island, but Chant was not concerned that the bulging slip covers or guns would be found; it would take an army to search the island, and Krowl knew it. He would focus his attention on finding the culprit.

As would the other torturers. They had to believe the

same thing—that one of their number was responsible. They would be cut off from one another, intensely suspicious, each man looking over his shoulder at the others, fearful that he could be the next victim.

The confusion, fear, and suspicion he had sown was all well and good, Chant thought—as long as it did not lead to Krowl's cancellation of his appointment with Viktor and Olga Petroff. But Chant was fairly confident that would not happen. If he read Krowl correctly, the torture doctor would, in the end, simply lock up the nine men and let them rot before he would forfeit what had to be for him his most important and challenging assignment.

Or so Chant hoped. In any case, there was nothing more to be done now but wait and see what happened—and try to survive for at least three more days.

No one came to see him for the rest of the day. Some time in what he judged to be late afternoon he heard the unmistakable *thwop-thwop-thwop* of helicopter rotors pass low overhead. The helicopter landed, but its engine was not shut off, and it took off again within minutes.

Reinforcements, Chant thought, perhaps specialists, or even—and the idea caused him to smile—torturers to torture the torturers. Of one thing he was certain, and that was that nobody would be leaving the island until one Krowl had found his records and the other had found his pearls.

He resisted the impulse to leave his cell again for another look outside, for he knew that whatever he saw wouldn't really matter. The new men Krowl had undoubtedly brought in changed the equation somewhat, but the problem—and his solution to it—remained the same. He was not foolish enough to think that Krowl would completely ignore him for three or four more days, and so he would find out what he needed to know eventually. And so he waited, resting with deep meditation, and occasionally slaking his thirst by licking condensation off the stone walls of the cell.

Finally he slept.

He was awakened by the rumble of the machinery behind the wall, the rattle of his chains. The chains retracted, inexorably pulling his body up on the wall, crucifying him.

Bernard came in a few minutes later. He was pushing the wheelchair with one hand, carrying a hypodermic needle in the other. He stopped in front of Chant, looked up, and drew his lips back from his teeth. Suddenly, without warning, he plunged the needle directly into the center of Chant's partially open bite wound. Chant bit off a scream and turned away as Bernard pressed the plunger on the hypodermic. Within moments, the drug had reached his brain and he passed out.

He awakened to find himself still in his cell, but strapped into the wheelchair. He was very thirsty. His tongue felt thick and furry, filling the back of his throat, and the wounds on his shoulder and stomach burned with a steady, searing heat. Bernard was leering in his face.

"You awake, Sinclair?"

"Would you believe me if I said no?"

"Did you miss me?"

"There are no words to express it."

"I guess that needle kind of hurt, huh?"

"You know, Bernard, you and I should fight some time. It isn't every day that one gets to spar with the world's champion professional karate fighter."

Bernard's smile vanished, and he straightened up. "You

may get your wish yet, Sinclair."

"I can hardly wait."

"I guarantee you'll regret it."

"Will you let me out of this wheelchair for the occasion?"

Bernard flushed angrily. "If my brother ever gave me permission to go one on one with you, you'd end up in a wheelchair permanently—if I didn't kill you. I'd tear your ass off, Sinclair. Then *I'd* have your rep."

"There's no one on earth I'd rather bequeath it to, Bernard. When can I look forward to this match?"

"My brother doesn't want you busted up—not yet."

"Doesn't he? You could have fooled me."

"You've got a smart mouth, Sinclair," Bernard said, abruptly stepping behind the wheelchair and pushing Chant forward, toward the open cell door. "That won't last much longer."

Chant was wheeled down the long corridor, through the swinging door to the outside. Then he was wheeled at a brisk pace up the incline toward the helicopter pad and the complex of buildings beyond.

On the lawn outside the dormitory, a number of trunks and suitcases had been gathered together and torn apart in an apparent search for false bottoms.

A number of broken people wandered listlessly through the brush, poking at the ground with sticks. One brown-uniformed guard stood at one of the entrances to the dormitory, and Chant assumed the second guard was standing by the other entrance.

Chant counted five new men, all dressed in black fatigues, and all carrying Uzis. One, a tall Japanese with piercing, intelligent black eyes, looked at Chant, then glanced quickly away.

"What's happening around here, Bernard?" Chant asked

easily. "It seems a little early for spring cleaning."

"Shut up, Sinclair." There was a pause, then: "You hear anything the other night?"

"What other night?"

"Last night."

"Nope. Slept like a baby. It must be the salt air. You have some kind of problem here, Bernard?"

"You're the one with the problem, Sinclair. And I told you to shut up."

Chant was wheeled into the windowless building, parked in front of Richard Krowl's desk. Krowl was uncharacteristically dressed in casual clothes—jeans and a heavy, white, cable-knit sweater that looked a size too big for him. He was unshaven, his pale eyes bloodshot and red-rimmed, with dark pouches beneath them.

Feather was also in the office, seated on the divan. She wore a large, hooded sweatshirt, with the hood over her head, covering her face, which was turned away.

"You don't look too good, Krowl," Chant said to the torture doctor. "The screaming around this place keeping you awake at night?"

"Why should you ask a question like that?" Krowl didn't smile, and his lids narrowed slightly.

Chant laughed. "I think you've been working yourself too hard in that torture chamber of yours. Too much research. I sit around for hours in my cell working up my best material, and it goes right over your head."

"Unhook the battery," Krowl said curtly to his brother, "and then get out."

Chant waited, but Bernard remained behind him, unmoving. "Let me work on this son of a bitch," Bernard said at last.

"Bernard . . . ?"

"You've got enough to worry about, Richard," Bernard continued, a note of obstinacy and resentment ringing clearly in his voice. "You've been fucking around with this wiseass long enough. When I finish beating the shit out of him, he'll be happy to tell you what you want to know. That'll be one less thing you have to worry about."

Richard Krowl's voice was low, slightly menacing. "Are you arguing with me, Bernard?"

"I'm just saying to your face what everybody else is saying behind your back. Just having this guy around spooks everybody. Now you're up to your ass in alligators here, and if you don't get things together real soon, you're going to be out of business."

"That would be rather unfortunate for you, Bernard," Richard Krowl said dryly. "Then you'd have to find a job."

"If the Russians find out what's going on here, they'll never—"

"Shut up, Bernard!" Krowl shouted. "And get out! I'll call you if I need you!"

Again, Chant sensed tremendous reluctance and resentment in the burly man standing behind him. Then Bernard grunted angrily, wheeled, and stalked out of the office.

Richard Krowl stared over Chant's shoulder at his departing brother, his eyes now cold, calculating. Finally, Krowl sighed, then reached beneath his desk and pressed a button. The steel cuffs on Chant's wrists popped open.

"The battery terminals are to your right," Krowl said almost absently. "I suggest you don't press on the arm of that chair too hard when you lean over."

Chant reached to his right beneath the chair, disconnected the battery terminals. "Are the Russians coming to visit?" he asked casually. "Frankly, that surprises me; they certainly have enough torture doctors of their own, and I wouldn't think they'd patronize an operation that seems to cater to your kinds of clients. They must think a lot of your skills."

Krowl said nothing. Feather, as usual, said nothing and

did not move. Krowl leaned back in his chair, folded his hands across his stomach and stared absently up at the ceiling.

Food and cold beer were brought. Chant ate and drank in silence, with Feather remaining motionless as a statue and Krowl continuing to stare at the ceiling.

"What's all the excitement around here?" Chant asked as he finished and set the tray down on the floor beside his wheelchair. "I thought I noticed some new faces on my way over. More students, Krowl?"

Now Krowl looked at Chant, sighed. "Sinclair, tell me about Operation Cooked Goose."

Chant shrugged. "I did. I got my shoulder burned for my effort."

"You lied."

Now Feather shifted her position on the divan, and when Chant glanced in her direction he found the woman looking at him. Her face, now visible under the hood, was badly swollen, and her right eye was almost shut. The left eye was fixed on a spot somewhere around his chest.

"What can I tell you, Krowl?" Chant said quietly as he continued to stare back at Feather. "I thought you were a scientist. Your machines indicated I told the truth. One shake of this woman's head, and I get burned. It doesn't make sense that you shouldn't believe me."

"It makes sense. Feather senses things no machine can; she sees into the human heart. She always knows."

"Not this time. I thought we agreed I didn't have any good reasons for continuing to resist."

"You chose to resist by different means—and considering the fact that you had my dim-witted brother waving a hot iron in your face, I don't blame you. The fact that you were able to pull it off with that iron in your face is what I find absolutely astounding. I've seen people beat lie detectors, but never for such a prolonged period of time, and never under such stress where a single mistake could have cost an eye, or worse. I wouldn't have thought it possible."

"It isn't possible. I told you the truth. I think your girlfriend here was off her feed."

"You lied—as you're doing now. You heard me tell the others how the human nervous system can be compared to a musical instrument that, when played properly, will produce the music you want to hear. You are the most unusual instrument I've ever come across. Indeed, you are probably unique. But I will learn to play you, John Sinclair. Whatever it takes, I will hear your music."

"Are those men in black outside your guest conductors?"

"No. As a matter of fact, they're mercenaries I've been forced to hire as temporary guards." Krowl paused for a few moments, staring hard into Chant's face. When he spoke again, his voice had taken on a sharper edge. "I have a problem, Sinclair. I think it may interest you."

"If you have a problem, Krowl, I know it will interest me. I hope it's a really big one."

"It's bothersome. It seems somebody on this island is a murderer and a thief."

Chant opened his eyes wide in mock horror and astonishment. "A thief and murderer *here?* I find that impossible to believe."

Krowl grunted, then lit a cigar and blew a smoke ring toward the ceiling. "Two guards are missing. Feather's jaw was broken. Two men were decapitated, and one was drowned in his own shit." The torture doctor's tone had become almost casual, conversational.

"Mmm," Chant said with a grimace. "Sounds gruesome. Any suspects?"

"Everybody on this island except the mercenaries, Feather, and myself."

Chant nodded toward the empty earthenware jars. "I see

your pearls are missing. Maybe the two guards did it."

Krowl shook his head. "They were fed to the sharks. Pieces of clothing were found floating in the lagoon. In any case, nobody can get on or off this island, except by helicopter—and nobody's going anywhere until I find the person responsible. That's why the problem is only bothersome, not critical."

"I'm really sorry to hear that. It sounds like Feather got off easily."

"Yes," Krowl said, squinting at Chant through a cloud of aromatic, blue smoke. "Curious, isn't it? It's almost as if this butcher were a man with some sense of honor who might have had some qualms about killing a woman."

Chant looked at Feather, smiled thinly. "Obviously, he'd never had any dealings with her." Shadows moved in the woman's good eye, and Chant looked back to Krowl; as always, the mute woman made him distinctly uneasy. "Maybe it's one of your guests."

"Yes, that could very well be. Something like this happened once before, although there weren't any killings involved. An agent for Amnesty, Inc., an investigator, got very brave and managed to get on this island posing as . . . someone else. He stole some records without my even being aware of it, and managed to leave with the group he'd come with. Fortunately, the theft was discovered. I did some quick checking, and my people were able to capture him in Peru before any damage had been done. I decided an example had to be made to discourage future interruptions of my work, so he was brought back here for special attention. His name was Harry Gray—the man who was in Vietnam the same time you were. I asked you about him. Do you still claim you didn't know him?"

"That's what I said."

Krowl looked at Feather, who gave a slight shrug of her shoulders.

"Feather isn't certain you're telling the truth," Krowl continued, turning back to Chant, raising his eyebrows slightly.

"If I were you, I'd trade her in on a new model. Why the hell would I lie about something like that?"

"An excellent question. But I haven't come to the most interesting part—actually, it's the reason I'm telling you all this."

"Oh, good. You've had more bad news?"

"I'll leave that for you to decide. Naturally, I suspected that I'd been infiltrated again, and that one of my guests was an agent for somebody."

"Why an agent? Maybe he's just a garden-variety madman."

"No. Again, records were taken."

Chant laughed. "Along with the pearls? He was really a busy beaver, wasn't he?"

"Oh, he certainly was. Naturally, my guests also suspected it was one of them—at first."

"At first?"

"Yes. But after their initial shock and panic wore off and they started talking with each other, they came up with another suspect. In fact, they're in unanimous agreement on who's responsible."

"Who?"

"You."

"I love it. You come up with some pretty good material yourself."

"It's not my material; it's theirs."

"Is this some kind of new interrogation technique, Krowl? If it is, I have to tell you that I prefer it to your other methods."

"Oh, they're quite serious. Indeed, I find their awe of you most intriguing. They talk about the strength, stealth, and cunning of the *ninja*. In fact, the thought of you wandering around at night lopping off heads and drowning strong men in their own shit so unhinged one of my guests —Chester Norham—that he demanded he be taken off the island immediately. When I told him that was impossible, he went back to his room and hanged himself with a bedsheet."

"Really? He never did have good nerves. Have you informed his mother?"

"Of course, it couldn't have been you," Krowl said around his cigar, still squinting through the smoke. His voice was flat. "No man, *ninja* or not, could walk away from shackles and through a locked door."

"Hey, I'd just as soon you didn't discourage their fantasies. Maybe a few more will hang themselves."

"Even assuming it was possible that you'd done it, it would seem logical for you to kill everyone."

"Frankly, I'm a bit disappointed that didn't seem logical to the person who did do the killings."

"You're disappointed, I'm curious," Krowl said in the same flat tone. "If it had been you, I'd have been the first victim on your list."

"I won't deny that."

"And, obviously, once you were free, with me in your power, it would have been insane for you to go back to your cell and return yourself to my power."

"That's for damn sure."

Krowl removed his cigar from his mouth, turned, and looked at Feather. The woman, who had been staring at Chant throughout the conversation, continued to stare at him, and she did not move.

"Tell me, Sinclair," the torture doctor said, abruptly changing the subject as he stood and stretched, "what would happen if you and Bernard fought?"

"With or without my wheelchair?"

"Would you be able to kill him, even after all I've put you through? If even a fraction of what I've heard about you in the last few days is true, it seems you actually could."

"Why don't we find out?"

"Perhaps we will."

"It sounds to me like you're trying to find a way to solve another of your problems, namely the aforementioned dim-witted brother."

"It's Bernard who keeps insisting he wants to beat the truth out of you."

"And it's you who may be looking to make him an object lesson to your pals. Bernard has a big mouth, and he has a natural kinship with those others. They like their brutality straight up, with none of the bullshit you're so fond of. The fact of the matter is that Bernard has been watching too many old Westerns; he thinks that if he knocks me off, he'll inherit what he perceives to be my reputation as top gunslinger."

"He's a killer, Sinclair."

"Sure he is—of people who weren't trying to kill him. Your brother is a coward, Krowl, and probably mildly retarded. He's big and brutal, but he's really a child who's wildly jealous of both of us, and is looking for a little attention. I'm telling you this up front, because I don't want to end up getting any extra-special attention because I've killed your brother in a game you set up. I've got enough grief trying to convince you and your human lie detector here that I've been telling the truth."

Krowl threw back his head and laughed. "You know, Sinclair," he said, still chuckling, "you really are a most amazing man. Most men would have been finished an hour or two after their arrival here. Here you are, days later, sitting here and warning of the consequences of possible acts. What's more, I *enjoy* our conversations. In fact, sometimes I enjoy them so much that I forget why it is you're here in the first place."

"Not to worry. I assume you taped everything I said, so you can play it back at your leisure. In the meantime, did you hear the one about—?"

"The tape is bullshit," Krowl said, suddenly very serious, his eyes glinting dangerously. "But you'll tell me the truth, eventually. That is, if Bernard doesn't kill you."

"Ah. You're still thinking that over, I see."

"Mmmm." Krowl puffed on his cigar, and his eyes once again became hooded. "In the meantime, I have this other aggravation to attend to. What would you do in my place, Sinclair? What do I do about this stray murderer and thief?"

"Why ask me?"

"I'm interested in your views."

"Why should I do your work for you?"

Krowl smiled thinly. "Because I have to assume that indulging me with this little chat beats hanging around in your cell, so to speak."

"What about Bernard? Maybe he went over the edge."

"And stole his own pearls?"

"The guards?"

"Most unlikely, but a possibility—for whatever reason. But I don't think so."

"Then you're left with your guests. Put them all under constant guard, search everything."

"Done."

"Get on the radio and have their respective governments do a thorough background check on every one of them. Make sure physical descriptions of the men they sent match up with the people you've got here."

"Done. Every description matches up, and each man is vouched for—in the strongest possible terms."

Chant shrugged. "Then one of them is either a maniac, or a deep-cover agent carrying out a careful plan which only seems crazy to us. Or maybe one of them had a grudge nobody knows about, and he stole the pearls and records to make it look like someone else."

"But what if my nervous guests are right, and it's you who's the murderer and thief?"

"There's a simple solution to that. Put me in chains inside a locked cell. That should make them feel better."

"What is this *ninja* business, Sinclair? Precisely what is a *ninja?*"

"Ask your guests."

"They describe you."

"How do they describe me?"

"As a man with almost supernatural powers."

"Do you believe in men with supernatural powers?"

"No. Not supernatural. But you are a man with demonstrably remarkable talents—and I've only observed you as a prisoner. To tell you the truth, the question of what you can and cannot do with your body and mind has come to intrigue me more than any other question we're supposed to be dealing with. I've come to look upon you as a great opportunity for learning that's literally been dumped in my lap."

"I hate to think that I'm distracting you from your work, Doctor. If it's all the same to you, I'd just as soon be ignored."

"But secrets of the body and mind—secrets that I believe you possess—are my business."

"Oh, yeah. I keep forgetting. For some reason, I keep thinking of you as a chickenshit torturer with delusions of grandeur."

Krowl puffed on his cigar, studying Chant, then abruptly dropped it on the floor of his office and ground it out with the toe of his shoe. "I'm going to be frank with you, Sinclair," the other man said at last, sitting back down behind his desk.

"Oh, please do."

"I'll find out who's responsible for this other business; it's only a matter of time. When I do find him, I'll do the same thing to him that I did to Harry Gray. However, it presents a problem because it couldn't have happened at a worse time."

"Why not?"

The torture doctor shook his head. "I'm not prepared to tell you that. But I am prepared to offer you a deal."

Chant grunted. "What's the deal?"

"Save me the time that your problem presents. Tell me what the Americans want to know; tell me the truth about any documents you may have, and give me a means of verifying what you tell me."

"I did tell you the truth."

"Don't give me that," Krowl said with an impatient wave of his hand. "Here's my proposition: Tell me what I want to know, and I won't kill you."

"I liked your other material better—the business about my walking away from my chains to wreak bloody vengeance and steal pearls, then going back again."

Krowl hissed with annoyance. "Of course, I could lie to you. But what would be the point? We've both agreed that, sooner or later, I'd get what I want from you."

"You have what you want; you just won't accept it."

"Sinclair, this is an honest offer."

"You can't release me," Chant said carefully. "If you did, the CIA would kill *you*."

"I didn't say I'd let you go free; I said I wouldn't kill you."

"Interesting proposition. But, as lovely as this island is, I suspect I might find it boring after a time."

"Are you admitting that you lied before?"

"You want to chat; I'm chatting. Like you said, I prefer it to hanging around on the wall of my cell."

"We won't be on this island." Now it was Richard Krowl's tone that was guarded."

"Where?"

"Russia."

Chant said nothing. He glanced at Feather, who was still staring, her unswollen eye slightly out of focus, at his chest.

"That caught you by surprise, didn't it?" Krowl said, more than a hint of satisfaction in his voice. "Would I make up such a thing? Maybe that will convince you that my offer is genuine."

"Why the hell do you want to go to Russia, Krowl? The food's terrible."

Another thin smile, a fresh cigar. "The Russians, in the past, haven't taken my work too seriously. They prefer their own rather crude methods—which work quite well for them under normal circumstances. But they're not fools, and they're certainly not a stupid people. They'd heard of my work, and from time to time they would send me subjects. They were impressed with my work. Now I've been given an unparalleled opportunity. If I pass one last . . . test . . . I'll be given unlimited access to the best facilities, as well as unlimited funds, in Russia to continue my research. That's always been the most important thing to me."

"Well, you'll certainly have no shortage of subjects to work on there," Chant said evenly. "You and the Russians will get on famously; you're both interested in absolute control of people."

"My work has scientific validity, Sinclair. Eventually, much good will come of it for all mankind. But to do the work, I've had to make compromises."

"You should learn to deliver that line with a German accent."

"Do you want to die?!"

"If I told you the truth about Cooked Goose, then I really would be a traitor, wouldn't I?"

"This is in your best interests, Sinclair. Remember, it was your countrymen who sent you here to be tortured and killed."

"What the hell do you really want from me, Krowl?"

"The secrets of the *ninja,"* Krowl said softly. "I want to know how you learned to control your autonomic nervous system and your emotions so well. I want to know how you elevate your tolerance for pain. There are many, many things I want to learn from you."

"I don't know what you're talking about, Krowl. You've been listening to too much of your guests' mumbo jumbo. Frankly, I'm surprised at your gullibility."

"Oh, but I've observed the wonders of your control first hand."

"I still don't know what you're talking about. I'm just a businessman who hasn't minded getting his hands dirty."

"Or bloody."

"That, too."

"Agree to cooperate with me—as my associate, if you will—and you can live."

"What about all the other people—the broken people—you have wandering around on this island? You going to take them to Russia, too?"

"No," Krowl said in a flat voice.

"You'll kill them?"

"Painlessly, yes—except for Feather. There's no other place for them to go, Sinclair. I'll be doing them a favor."

"There are organizations, other facilities. For Christ's sake—"

"I can't leave tracks like that, Sinclair. If anything that's happened here could be *proven,* it might forever jeopardize publication of my research findings. What's been done can't be undone—but it can be forgotten, if it's allowed to be. Then, in ten or fifteen years, the Russians can slowly begin to publish my work. I'll be dead in fifty years, but my work will live on. When the whole story is known, and when it can be viewed dispassionately, the world will be able to understand the great value of my work."

Chant nodded toward Feather. "What's her story?"

The woman shook her head ever so slightly, but if it was a sign of disapproval, Krowl paid no attention to it.

"Maria was camp physician with a group of guerillas fighting Somoza, in Nicaragua," the torture doctor declared matter-of-factly. "She was captured by Somoza's soldiers, who, naturally, wanted to know the location of the camp and the names of other guerilla leaders. Maria refused to talk, and so she was tortured out in the jungle. The soldiers were unsophisticated, and they began by burning Maria's genitals with a flaming brand."

Chant groaned inwardly. "I'm sorry," he murmured to the woman, who had bowed her head. Her shoulders sagged.

"Maria would have told them what they wanted to know," Krowl continued in the same matter-of-fact tone, "but she was in too much agony to speak. Her torturers mistook this for reluctance, and they redoubled their efforts, actually inserting the brand up into her vulva and womb. She passed out frequently, but she was never given time to recover—to catch her breath, so to speak, so that she could talk. As soon as Maria woke up, they went to work on her again. All Maria could do was scream . . . and after a time she stopped doing even that. Finally her torturers gave up and left her for dead, which she might as well have been. She was found by her companions and nursed back to something approximating physical health, but her mind appeared to be completely gone. She could not walk, talk, or even feed herself. She was catatonic, totally unable to care for herself, just a breathing lump of flesh.

"During those years, I was a research neurologist who was part of a team studying the treatment of multi-damaged, psychologically disoriented trauma victims—like Maria. When the Sandinistas defeated Somoza and took over the government, Maria was sent to us for evaluation and possible treatment. Because of the extensive physical damage that had been done to her, I was put in charge of her case.

"To get right to the point, extensive reconstructive surgery was considered pointless; the psychiatrists deemed her hopelessly catatonic, her mind completely gone. I wondered. In fact, I wondered what her reaction might be—and if there were any reaction at all, the psychiatrists would have been amazed—if she were given the opportunity to torture her torturers, or one of them. It so happened that the opportunity was available; Maria's chief torturer was well known to the Sandinistas, and they had him in prison. I made contact with certain individuals in the government, and they indicated their complete willingness to . . . make the individual available to me."

"I take it you didn't bother informing your colleagues, or the medical school, of your plans?"

"Of course not. The experiment would have been disapproved immediately, and I considered the chance of helping Maria to be more important than the approval of my colleagues."

"Bullshit, Krowl. The idea of playing torturer turned you on."

"History will act as my judge, Sinclair, not you!" Krowl snapped. "You see the results before you."

"I'm not sure what I see before me," Chant said quietly, cocking his head and looking directly at the bowed head of Feather.

"She began to respond when I simply *told* her of the arrangements that were being made. The day after I spoke with her, she ate by herself for the first time since she'd been found. She was told that he would be totally under her control, and that she could do with him what she wanted, for as long as she wanted. I told her I would provide her with whatever she wanted. Two days later she handed me a drawing—of a feather. I got it for her, and I made arrangements for her to visit her torturer, held in a soundproofed room inside the consulate of a government friendly to the Sandinistas, at her convenience. I learned a great deal from watching those sessions, Sinclair. Maria is a woman with considerable skill, intelligence . . . and imagination. She killed the man using nothing but that single feather. It took him almost seven weeks to die. She was very patient with him."

Chant remembered the agony of the one night Feather had spent with him, shuddered involuntarily. "Then, I take it, the med school got wind of what you were doing?"

Krowl nodded. "I was dismissed, and my license to practice taken away."

"I'm surprised you weren't prosecuted."

"There would have been a trial, and all parties agreed that the medical school wouldn't benefit by being written up on the front pages of every scandal sheet in the country. The charges against me were dropped, in exchange for my agreement to leave the country and never practice medicine anywhere in the world again. So I left, and I took Feather with me."

"That alone makes you a son of a bitch, Krowl."

"Maria chose to come with me."

"Of course, she chose to come with you. You'd provided her with a bridge to reality. At that point, you should have given her over to people who could have continued her treatment."

"There was, and is, no other treatment. In order for Feather to be able to function at all, she must be in a situation where she is allowed to administer both agony and ecstasy."

"Who says?"

"I say."

"Who have you consulted? Amnesty, Inc. runs programs that—"

"There are no programs that will help Feather. And I don't have to consult anybody; *I'm* the one who should be consulted, for I am now the leading expert in this field."

"I'll tell you what you are, Krowl, and I don't have to consult anyone to know it. You're a fucking nut case. This whole island is one huge pornography parlor for you, and I'll bet you jerk off a dozen times a day. It's too bad Chester hung himself. Once the two of you had gotten to know each other better, you really would have enjoyed jerking each other off."

Chant's words had been carefully calculated to create an explosion—to disrupt, disturb, confuse, and distract. But Krowl's reaction surprised him. The torture doctor sat in silence, staring at Chant. Strange shadows—sadness, perhaps, or guilt, or confusion—passed across the man's pale green eyes. Finally he looked away. His voice, when he spoke, was barely above a whisper.

"If you wish to live, you will accompany me to Russia. You will share your training with me, cooperate in tests I will design. You will voluntarily share the secrets of your remarkable mind and body in exchange for your life. What do you say?"

Time. Two more days.

Chant sighed resignedly. "I'm tired, Krowl," he said

evenly. "You've given me an honest proposal, so I'll give you an honest answer. Give me a day or so in peace to think about it. It sounds like an offer I can't refuse, but I have to be certain in my own mind that I can live with it; otherwise, I won't be able to give you what you want."

Immediately, Krowl swung around in his chair, leaned forward, and rested his hand on Feather's bowed back. More than a minute passed, and then the woman slowly shook her head.

"Too bad," Krowl said with a sigh. He opened his top desk drawer, withdrew a machine pistol, which he aimed at Chant's head. "Feather says you lie; you have no intention of cooperating with me, now or in the future. Please place your arms back on the armrests of the wheelchair."

Chant did as he was told. Krowl pushed the button beneath the desk, and the wrist cuffs snapped back into place.

"It's a real pity that you're so stubborn, Sinclair," the man with the long blond hair and pale green eyes continued softly. "But then, I suppose that's just one part of the power you have that intrigues me so much. I *will* learn the secrets of that power; I will learn to play you. You could have saved yourself a lot of agony, and you'll be accompanying me to Russia in any case. For now . . . ? Perhaps another visit from Feather will help you to reconsider your bad attitude."

"You're a tough audience, Dr. Gonzalez," Chant said quietly to the woman. When she did not respond or look up, Chant turned his attention back to Krowl. "For an administrator who lost two guards, three guests, your records, and a fortune in pearls last night, and then had another guest hang himself this morning, you seem remarkably sanguine and relaxed about it all."

Krowl seemed genuinely amused. "Do I? Maybe I'm learning something from you."

"Krowl, your fixation on me in the light of your other

problems strikes me as positively unhealthy."

"Sure, but you've already told me how unhealthy I am."

"I don't mean to tell you your business, but don't you think you should be devoting more attention to catching your in-house Jack the Ripper?"

"Oh, but I told you I'll find the person responsible. Where is he going to go? There is no one else on the island but us, and no one will be going anywhere until he is found out and the missing items recovered. I have my new guards to watch the old guards, and all of them to keep the others under constant surveillance until I decide which individual to start working on first. So, you see, there really is no problem, at least certainly nothing to keep me from proceeding with the other business at hand—you."

"I'm really sorry to hear that."

"You're going to be even sorrier." Krowl pressed a switch on his desktop intercom. "Bernard?"

Bernard's surly response came over the loudspeaker above Chant's head. *"Yeah?"*

"Bernard, do you still want to fight John Sinclair? He indicates that killing you would hardly cause him to work up a sweat."

"Give him to me, Richard." Bernard's voice hummed with rage and tension. *"Ten minutes; that's all I ask. Give me ten minutes with him, and he'll tell you everything you want to know."*

"That's enormously reassuring, Bernard," Krowl said dryly, glancing at Chant out of the corners of his eyes. "Have the guards gather everyone out by the helicopter pad. Then you may come and fetch Mr. Sinclair. He's all yours."

EIGHTEEN

"BERNARD," CHANT SAID easily as the burly, crew-cut man came to get him, "your brother's looking for a way to get rid of you. He's planning on going to Russia, and he probably knows you won't want to make the trip. He also won't want to leave you behind, since he could never be sure who you might end up talking to. He's counting on my killing you. How do you feel about that?"

Bernard, startled, glanced around at his brother, who was leaning casually against his desk, the machine pistol in one hand, and the other hand thrust into the pocket of his jeans. Feather, head still bowed and shoulders slumped, stood silently beside him.

Richard Krowl shrugged. "If you want to fight him, take him outside where we can all watch. If you want to hear him whisper sweet nothings in your ear, take him back to his cell and let me get on with other business."

Bernard flushed purple. He stepped around behind the wheelchair, yanked it around and pushed Chant out of the office. Chant was wheeled outside and down a concrete walk toward the helicopter pad and the assemblage that had been gathered in a large circle on the grass around it. It appeared to Chant that everyone on the island had been brought to the site. There were half a dozen of the strange, white-haired broken people, the two brown-uniformed guards, and the ominous-looking, black-uniformed mercenaries with their Uzis.

The circle parted slightly as they approached. Chant was wheeled to the center, turned around. Bernard, glaring at Chant, removed his shirt, shoes, and socks as his brother stood next to the wheelchair and addressed the group.

"Well," Krowl said wryly, "now we're going to have a break from this other nasty unpleasantness while Bernard provides us with some entertainment. We're going to have a martial arts demonstration."

There were murmurs from the eight remaining torturers, and they exchanged surprised glances. Eyes that were glassy from fear and lack of sleep came alive in their pasty faces.

"But there is a more serious purpose," Krowl continued in a sharper tone. "All but one of you came here to learn from me, but perhaps it is I who shall learn from you. In the last few days, I have noted mounting disagreement among many of you concerning my handling of John Sinclair. You, I take it, would prefer a more sustained and brutal approach. Bernard, as you all know, agrees with you. He's told me he will beat the information we want out of the prisoner. For his own reasons of pride, he wishes to do this with no restraints on the prisoner. Now, perhaps, I'll discover that you were right all along."

There was more murmuring among the torturers, and a

few loud expressions of dissent. The men started to step back, stopped when two of the black-uniformed guards raised their machine guns slightly. Chant scanned the faces before him, smiled.

"It's absolutely amazing," Krowl said, and laughed. "I'm certainly looking forward to this demonstration. After all, I've heard so much from you about John Sinclair's fighting skills that I want to see for myself. Now I see that you don't share my enthusiasm, even though he's exhausted, seriously weakened, and has painful wounds on his belly and shoulder. I'm almost sorry I didn't follow Bernard's advice and have this demonstration earlier, before so much of Mr. Sinclair's strength had been drained away."

"Let's get on with it, Richard," Bernard growled in a low, tense voice. "I want to get at this bastard."

Krowl turned to the tall Japanese with the bright eyes. "Direct your men to shoot Mr. Sinclair in the legs if he tries to run away, or if it looks as if he means to attack anyone but Bernard. I don't want him dead, but you may cripple him."

"You have already told them," the Japanese replied evenly, in perfect English.

Richard Krowl removed what appeared to be a tiny radio transmitter from his back pocket. He pressed a button on the device, and the cuffs restraining Chant's wrists and ankles snapped open. Chant slowly rose from the chair, stretched his muscles, cracked his joints, then stepped away from the chair and stood in the center of the circle, arms hanging loosely from his sides, a thin smile on his face as he looked at the bare-chested man standing a few yards away.

"Come and die, Bernard," Chant said softly.

Bernard went down into a fighting stance, inched forward. He expected the other man to adopt a stance, but the man with the cold, iron-colored eyes simply stood still, waiting for him in the center of the circle.

More than anything, Bernard had wanted to fight this man, defeat him, kill him. More than anything, Bernard had wanted to be known as the man who had killed John Sinclair. But now, standing in the circle free of shackles and out of the wheelchair, John Sinclair seemed so much bigger. . . .

"Bernard?" Richard Krowl had taken Chant's place in the wheelchair and had wheeled himself to a position next to the tall Japanese. He was sitting with one leg casually crossed over the other, the machine pistol resting in his lap. "We're all waiting for you. Is this going to take all day?"

He had wanted to be taken seriously by his brother, to be respected by other men as well as feared. He had seen himself gaining these things by defeating John Sinclair. Now, as he stared into the other man's cold eyes, all he saw was his own death. He straightened up, took a step back. . . .

Richard Krowl absently scratched his temple with the barrel of the machine pistol. "Bernard? Could we get on with it? You can hardly expect Mr. Sinclair to come to you, since you're the one who's threatened to tear his ass off."

"That's all right," Chant said evenly as he stepped forward. "I'll be happy to go to Bernard."

"I'm not going to fight him!" Bernard shouted, quickly stepping backward.

Chant stopped, waited. "What's the problem, Bernard?"

"Yes, Bernard," Richard Krowl said, leaning forward in the chair, "what is the problem?"

"His problem," one of the torturers, a Korean, said, "is that he's about to shit in his pants."

All of the torturers began to laugh, and smiles touched even the faces of the black-uniformed guards.

Now he had to fight, Bernard thought as his face grew

fiery hot. He could not let them laugh at him. He would leap forward, aim a side kick at the wound on the other man's belly, follow with a blow to the seared shoulder. The other man was just putting on a show; he was hurt, weak. Defeating him now would be easy, if only he could get himself to move. . . .

The other man would kill him, Bernard thought. For reasons he did not understand, he was absolutely certain of that. He did not want to die.

"Look at him!" Bernard shouted, pointing toward Chant's stomach, feeling the others' laughter washing over him like a physical force, a wave of boiling water. "The guy's bleeding, and with that burn on his shoulder, he won't even be able to lift his arm. I'm not going to have it be said about me that I was able to whip John Sinclair just because he was half-dead! I'll wait until he's stronger!"

As if in response, Chant swung his left arm in a complete circle.

"Bernard," the torture doctor said with a sigh, "I think Mr. Sinclair is quite willing to fight you now. As you well know, it's questionable whether the man will live much longer, much less get stronger. You said you wanted to fight this man so that you could show us what you could do. I suggest you take this opportunity; there may not be another."

Bernard, his entire body trembling and his face crimson with rage and shame, wheeled and pushed his way through the circle.

"That's too bad," Krowl said. "I really did want to see a demonstration of Mr. Sinclair's legendary martial arts skills." He paused, looked up at the tall Japanese. "What about you? You and your men are all supposed to be martial arts experts. You people are costing me a small fortune. How about earning your pay? Will you fight Sinclair?"

"It's not what I'm being paid for," the Japanese replied

simply. "You said nothing about giving exhibitions."

"You're paid to do what I ask you to."

"We were hired to provide security. If he attacks you, I will shoot him in the legs—as you instructed."

"Are you afraid of him?"

The other man did not reply.

It was to his advantage to fight, Chant thought. The more impressed and intrigued the torture doctor was by his physical skills, the less likely Krowl was to do anything that would cause him permanent physical damage.

"Will you fight me?" Chant asked in Japanese, addressing the tall, keen-eyed leader of the mercenaries.

"No, *Sensei,*" the Japanese replied in his own language.

"Do you know me?"

"I know of you. This man and his brother are assholes."

Chant suppressed a smile. "Are you a torturer, like these others?"

"No, *Sensei*. And I am not a fool. I am good enough to know my limitations."

"Then you must be very good, indeed."

"I will not go up against you."

"I would be honored to fight with you—but not to the death. I understand that the services of you and your men are contracted for, but in this case my interests and those of your employer are the same. Will you spar with me?"

"If this asshole wants."

"Ask him. Then pick two others—your best."

Richard Krowl, who had been listening to the two men converse in Japanese with an air of bemusement, now raised his machine pistol off his lap, looked at Chant, and raised his eyebrows slightly. *"Que pasa, hombre?"* There was more than a hint of nervousness in his voice.

"You wanted a fight," Chant replied easily. "I've just arranged it."

"Not to the death," the Japanese said in English.

Krowl nodded. "Good. Death isn't what I'm looking for at the moment. Sinclair, how many languages do you speak?"

"Enough to enable me to get around."

"What else were the two of you talking about?"

"It takes a long time to arrange a fight in Japanese."

"Give me your gun," Krowl said to the Japanese, moving his own machine pistol ever so slightly in the man's direction. The Japanese did as he was told, and Krowl grunted. "Could you kill this man in a no-holds-barred fight? He's been through a lot in the past few days. He can't be the same man he used to be."

"John Sinclair is a great *sensei,*" the Japanese replied simply. "A warrior . . . and sometimes a teacher."

"That may be," Krowl said, "but I'm the one paying you. I wouldn't want that to slip your mind."

"You purchased my skills and gun, and those of the men under my command. You didn't buy my respect."

"Hey, now—"

"The *sensei* has suggested that he spar against me and two of my men. Is this your wish?"

Krowl thought about it, nodded his head. "Go ahead," he said, and pointed his own gun at Chant's legs.

The Japanese motioned to two of his men, a black and a caucasian, and they handed their guns to other mercenaries before stepping out into the circle. The Japanese spoke to them. All three men bowed to Chant, who bowed back, then flexed his knees slightly as the men split and began to circle him.

The black and the caucasian on his flanks attacked first, a split second apart, one throwing a high kick at his head and the other a roundhouse kick at his midsection. Chant spun counterclockwise, parrying the high kick with his forearm, avoiding the roundhouse, then catching the Japanese with a straight arm blow to the chest that would have killed the other man if it had been thrown with full force. He came back under a blow thrown by the black, flipped him in the air with a judo throw, then rolled at the white's legs, knocking him off his feet. Instantly, Chant was back on his feet, crouched and ready.

There were grunts of surprise from the onlookers, and even Richard Krowl nodded his head slightly in appreciation. Only Feather stood, as always, mute and unmoving—although her eyes were directed toward the men in the center of the ring.

Chant and his opponents bowed to each other once again, and the bout resumed—a graceful but incredibly quick ballet of violence with spinning and flying bodies that would have been marked by blood, broken bones, and death if the punches and kicks had not been pulled.

Even as Chant fought, his gaze would occasionally flick to the faces of the men in the circle. Suddenly Bernard, his face still flushed, appeared in the circle, shoving his way in between one of the broken people and a brown-uniformed guard. A large blade flashed in his right hand—and the burly man charged, pushing aside one of Chant's black-uniformed opponents, who was just getting to his feet after being thrown.

Chant spun away from blows thrown by the Japanese and the black, who had not yet seen Bernard. Instead of coming back at the men with counterblows, Chant continued the momentum of his spin, then suddenly left his feet. His body whipped around in the air with almost blinding speed as he spun clockwise; halfway through the spin his right leg came out, and his bare heel smashed into Bernard's face with crushing force. Blood and teeth sprayed over the faces of those onlookers closest to Bernard as the burly man slowly spun around, then sat down hard, his hands over the broken lower part of his face.

Silence.

Chant's black-uniformed opponents bowed slightly, stepped back into the circle. Bernard, blood streaming through his cupped hands, began to softly moan in pain, shock, and disbelief. Chant stepped forward, gripped Bernard under the left elbow, brought him up to his feet. He effortlessly slung the man over his shoulders, then turned to his left and moved his head. Two torturers quickly moved aside, forming a break in the ring. Chant, with the moaning Bernard slung over his shoulders, stepped out of the ring and moved off down the walk to his right, heading for the shark lagoon.

A few seconds later Chant heard the soft, mechanical whisper of the wheelchair gaining on him. He did not stop or turn. Richard Krowl casually rode down the incline past him, used his hands to brake, then turn the chair to face Chant. The machine pistol came up, aimed at Chant's thighs, and Chant stopped.

"That's far enough, Sinclair," the torture doctor said in a flat voice.

"I'm on garbage detail, Krowl—doing your dirty work for you. You want him dead, I'll get him dead. I could have killed him back there instead of just knocking his teeth out. I prefer to feed him to the sharks."

"Ah, yes, but it would look tacky if I let you do that. Put him down—or I'll put a bullet in your leg."

Chant abruptly shrugged Bernard off his shoulders, but he kept a steel grip on the man's right wrist, holding it firmly in position as the man fell; the wrist snapped with an audible crack, and Bernard shrieked in agony.

"Gee, I'm really sorry about that," Chant said evenly, glancing back and forth between the torture doctor in the wheelchair and Bernard, who was continuing to wail and spray blood from his mouth as he writhed on the ground, cradling his shattered wrist to his chest. "I should have put him down more carefully."

Krowl did not even glance at his brother as he got out of the chair, stepped well back, then motioned with the machine pistol for Chant to sit down.

"Take him back to his cell and chain him," Krowl said to the two black-uniformed guards who had come up and now flanked Chant, the muzzles of their Uzis jammed into his ribs. "Take two other men with you. If he resists, shoot him in both kneecaps. Unless Mr. Sinclair changes his attitude very quickly, he's not going to have any need of his legs anyway."

NINETEEN

AT SUNDOWN, THE machinery behind the wall began to whine. The chains retracted, inexorably pulling Chant up on the cold stone, pinning him there.

Feather came to him an hour later.

A key rattled in the lock. The cell door swung open and Feather, silent as death, glided through the dim light cast by the overhead fixtures, stopping a yard away from him. She was dressed in jeans, sneakers, and a cotton blouse, and wore a green scarf wrapped around her head to partially hide her swollen face.

Slowly, her head tilted back and she looked directly into Chant's face with her slightly out-of-focus eyes. She stood like that for what seemed a very long time to Chant, and he felt his stomach muscles tighten. A chill started at the base of his skull, flickered down his body.

She knew, Chant thought; she knew he had done the killing.

"Hello, Maria," Chant said softly.

The olive-skinned woman with the huge, soulful, dark eyes slowly unbuttoned her blouse, shrugged it off her shoulders to the floor. She wore no bra, and her large, firm breasts glistened slightly with perspiration, although it was not warm in the cell. She reached behind her, withdrew from her jeans pocket a large, white feather with a shaft that was still stained with his blood.

She knew it had been him who had attacked her.

But she had not told Richard Krowl. He was also sure of that.

"You're a healer, Doctor," Chant continued in the same quiet voice. "At least, you were once. What you do here is evil. Certainly, some of us deserve the agony you bring us—but not all. Some of us are like you were when you were captured by the soldiers."

Sweat formed high on her chest, rolled down the cleft between her breasts. Her hand came up, softly brushed his belly with the fronds of the feather. Chant's flesh quivered.

"You were terribly, terribly hurt, Maria." Already, his lungs were beginning to ache, and he drew in a deep breath. "You were hurt beyond what anyone else can imagine. In a very real sense, you died out in that jungle. Part of you was resurrected when you tortured to death the man who had tortured you. What you did then was just; what you do now, acting as house torturer for Krowl, is not."

Slowly, the woman undid the rest of his coveralls to expose his genitals. She put her hand on him, hesitated, then began to stroke his penis.

"You have become your own enemy—*ah!*"

She had stabbed him in the belly with the shaft of the feather, just below his bite wound. Chant gasped for breath, swallowed hard. There had been something different about that particular strike, he thought; there had been emotion in it, as opposed to the calculated manner in which she had taken him apart before. She was angry with him—or wanted him to stop talking.

"You don't have to hurt others to feel alive any longer, Maria," Chant said through clenched teeth, feeling the fronds of the feather softly—menacingly—stroking the stiff shaft of his penis. Sweat had now begun to flow freely off both their bodies. "There can be an end to this nightmare—if you want an end—*ah!* Listen—*ah!*—to me. There are people who can help you. You can be healed all the way. Nobody can ever make up for what was done to you, but you can be whole again. There is reconstructive surgery that can erase the scars, open the passages that were burned shut. If you can't have a child, then you can adopt one. You can know love again, feel good again . . ."

Chant paused and grimaced when she began to poke at his testicles and the tip of his penis with the shaft of the feather.

"Help me," Chant groaned through his agony. "Fight back, Maria. Krowl only gave back a part of you—the part that he wanted. You can take back the rest of you. This is a living nightmare you must will yourself to wake from. If you help me, I can help you; as ridiculous as that may sound, it's true. Perhaps you know it's true, for you were spared the other night. If you help me, if you don't harm me anymore, I can take you to people who can heal the rest of you—body and mind. You are a beautiful woman, Maria. You can live again. You don't have to hurt any longer. Stop. Be a healer again."

Trying to speak while hanging from the wall was taking its toll, and Chant paused to gasp for breath. He sucked in a deep breath and steeled himself for agony when he saw the woman's hand come up, shaft pointing forward, to strike him in the genitals. The hand froze, slowly dropping back to her side. With the other hand, she pushed back the scarf, then raised her face and looked at him. She looked directly into his eyes. For the first time, her own eyes were in focus.

Tears glistened in those eyes, rolled down her cheeks.

Dr. Maria Gonzalez picked up her blouse, turned, and walked across the cell. She paused, pressed a stone near the door. The machinery behind the wall began to whir, and the chains to loosen. The woman called Feather turned to look at him once again, then abruptly walked from the cell, leaving the door open.

A reprieve, Chant thought as he was lowered to the floor of the cell. But for how long? The woman was, to say the least, emotionally unstable, and an unpredictable ally. She could spare him pain, but she could not buy him the time he needed. Only he could do that. He needed one to two more days. Since Krowl had given every indication that virtually nothing would cause him to warn off the Russians, Chant knew that he had a greater range of options—or two options, really. He could stay in his cell and wait, hope that he would still be in one piece and able to think and function when the Petroffs were brought to the island.

Or he could attack—disrupt, confuse, distract. Again.

Within two minutes Chant was free of his shackles, out of the cell and standing at the swinging doors, peering through a crack. He had expected at least one guard to be posted outside the cellblock this time, but there was not; despite Krowl's probing, the torture doctor had not taken seriously the suggestion that a shackled man inside a locked cell could be the marauder. Richard Krowl had obviously decided to concentrate all his forces around the main complex of buildings, and this could not have pleased Chant more.

Chant slipped out through the sliding doors. There was

a full moon in a cloudless sky, and Chant took a circuitous route, hiding in the shadows of the cellblock building, then darting across a small open space behind the building to the safety of a stand of trees and low brush. He worked his way carefully and silently through the brush, around the perimeter of the cleared area. Twenty minutes later he had reached the main complex, and was crouched in the shadows of the radio shack, applying dirt to his hands, feet, and face.

One brown-uniformed guard who had been stationed in the brush near the helicopter pad lay dead back there, his neck broken and his body covered with dry leaves. Also, Chant knew just about where every other guard was; there was one on the roof, one at each of the entrances. That left Bernard, one brown-uniformed guard, and two of the mercenaries; and Chant was almost certain that one of them would be acting as Richard Krowl's personal bodyguard. That left only two guards unaccounted for, and Chant could only hope they were not wandering the grounds, perhaps checking his cell. . . .

The huge radio antenna soared into the night sky close to the dormitory building, and this was the route Chant took to get to the roof, climbing hand over hand inside the skeleton shadows of the steel superstructure.

The guard on the roof was a mercenary—not marked for death by Chant. Chant waited, crouched on a cross girder inside the antenna superstructure three feet from the roof, until the man in the black uniform turned to light a cigarette, shielding the match from the wind blowing at his back. In an instant, Chant had leaped from the antenna to the roof and delivered a hard blow to the back of the man's neck. Chant was already across the roof and through the maintenance access door in the center by the time the mercenary's unconscious body had slumped to the pebbly, oiled surface.

Chant silently descended a short staircase, paused behind the door at the bottom and peered through a small window at the dimly lit corridor of the dormitory's third floor. A mercenary, one of the men Chant had sparred with earlier in the day, was patrolling the corridor. The man paused at the opposite end of the corridor, and for a moment Chant thought the man would descend the stairs to the second floor. He did not. The man turned and headed back, stopping to listen with his ear to the door of each room.

The mercenary was good, Chant thought—alert and conscientious. That meant he was going to have to be even better; if he wasn't, he was going to end up dead—or worse.

Chant waited until the man was a few paces away from the door, then he crouched in the stairwell—and scratched at the bottom of the door while he fixed his gaze on the light at the crack at the bottom. He waited a count of ten, then scratched again.

Suddenly two shadows—feet—appeared on the thin bar of light. Chant shoved the door open hard, catching the guard on the chest, driving him backward. Instantly, Chant was through the door, snatching the machine gun away with his left hand while his right fist smashed into the man's jaw.

Chant caught the man under the arm, eased him down to the floor, then crouched and listened. The sounds of this struggle had been unavoidable, but as far as Chant could tell, no one had heard. He waited almost thirty seconds, but the only sound he heard was a faint snoring coming from the room just across the hall.

That was where he went, using his lock pick to open the door, making his way by moonlight spilling in through the windows across the sitting room and into the bedroom.

Chant awoke the Korean torturer, gave the man just

enough time to recognize him in the moonlight, then smashed his larynx with a blow from the side of his hand delivered across the man's throat. The man screamed soundlessly, gagging and thrashing. With his left hand planted firmly on the man's chest, holding him in place, Chant brought the side of his right hand down across the bridge of the man's nose, snapping it cleanly. Then he changed the angle of his swing, knifing his hand horizontally through the air at the man's nose, driving the broken bone splinters up into the man's brain, killing him instantly.

There was no guard on the second floor. Chant killed his second victim with a neck slash from a straight razor he found in the bathroom.

He awoke his third victim with a devastating punch to the groin. As the man, a burly Argentine, sat bolt upright in bed, gasping for breath and thrusting his hands between his legs, Chant shoved him back down again—using a toilet plunger clapped over the man's nose and mouth. The man died in less than a minute, sucking for air in a foul-smelling vacuum.

Then Chant returned to his cell the way he had come. Everything was as he had left it. He locked the cell door, wired his lock pick back in place on the chain near his right hand, snapped the shackles shut on his wrists and ankles.

TWENTY

THE FIRST FACE he saw in the morning indicated to Chant that he had lost his gamble, and was about to die.

There was no time to arm the ultimate weapon that was in his mind and body—and no need, no point; the mindless rage in Bernard Krowl's eyes indicated to Chant that death would come quickly, despite the gruesome possibilities offered by the hunting knife in the man's good hand.

"I don't know what the fuck is going on around this place, Sinclair," the man with the short hair and pink scalp growled as he stepped into the cell and immediately slapped the stone on the wall to his right. "Three more guys were butchered here last night. I don't know who the fuck is doing it, but I'm sure as hell going to kill you before somebody kills me. I'm going to skin you alive, you son of a bitch."

Chant had reached across his body for his pick the moment Bernard had entered the cell—but he was too late. He managed to undo the wire, but before he could get a firm grasp on the pick, his hands were pulled apart by the retracting chains. The pick fell to the floor, rattling around with a series of loud metallic clicks before it finally came to rest.

Bernard did not even seem to notice the dropped pick—or he did not care. The broken, toothless, lower part of his face was wired in place, making his words muffled and mushy but strangely amplified by hatred and rage. His shattered wrist was in a cast inside a sling draped around his neck. He was obviously in great pain, his every word and movement now fueled by hate.

As Chant was pulled up and pinned on the wall, Bernard stepped close and pressed the point of the hunting knife to Chant's lower belly, breaking the skin and drawing blood.

"Did you hear what I said, asshole?" Bernard continued. The effort, his need, to talk caused the wires holding his jaw together to cut through the gums, and blood ran from his lips. "I'm going to skin you, strip by strip."

"Uh, have you talked to your big brother about this, Bernard?"

"Fuck him. Let him try pasting you back together again when I get finished with you."

"Bernard, you seem cranky this morning," Chant said evenly, keeping his eyes directly on Bernard's face as Feather, silent as always, suddenly appeared behind Bernard, in the doorway of the cell. She was holding her bloodstained feather like a knife in her right hand, and Chant raised his voice slightly as she suddenly started walking forward. "Why don't you go back to your place and have another cup of coffee? You'll feel better. Then you and I can sit down and talk this thing over."

"We'll see how funny you feel when I get finished with you, Sinclair," Bernard mumbled, and started to draw the blade down through Chant's flesh.

Feather came up directly behind Bernard and without hesitation swung the feather around and jabbed the sharpened shaft into his right ear.

Bernard howled in pain and surprise. He dropped the knife, clasped both hands to his ruined ear, then reeled halfway around and dropped to his knees. His high-pitched wailing went even higher as Feather pierced his left eye. Blood spurted, splashed over the stone floor.

"Get out of here," Chant said to the woman as she turned and walked back to the doorway, where she pressed the stone on the wall. The chains began to come out of the wall, lowering Chant to the floor of the cell. "With all that racket he's making, everyone on the island is going to be here. Go now, Maria!

Feather, as if paralyzed, stayed where she was as the chains continued to come out of the wall with agonizing slowness. Chant knew better than to waste energy pulling on them; there was nothing he could do but wait until he was lowered to the floor and there was sufficient slack to enable him to get to the pick, fifteen feet away.

But Bernard was not finished yet. The sound of the whirring machinery and clanking chains cut through his screams, reaching a place in his mind even deeper than his shock and agony. He stopped screaming and looked up, fixing Chant with his good eye. Then he began searching with his hands for the knife.

The machinery continued to whir, Chant continued to be lowered . . . slowly. The balls of his feet were now on the floor, giving him some leverage.

But Bernard had the knife. He staggered, raised the knife over his head, and rushed at Chant. Chant was able to bring his right arm up just far enough to deflect the blade with the wrist shackle. Sparks flew. Bernard dropped to his knees, then slowly struggled to his feet for another charge.

Then Feather was on him, stabbing at his head with the quill point of her strange weapon. Bernard wheeled to slash at her, but in doing so stepped very close to Chant. Chant wrapped one slack chain around the man's neck, snapped it with a single, quick tug. Bernard died with his eyes bulging nearly out of their sockets.

"Now get out of here!" Chant shouted at the woman. "Damn you, Maria, get out of here!"

But it was too late. The tall Japanese and two of his men suddenly rushed into the cell, their Uzis held at the ready. The bright eyes of the Japanese took in everything at a glance—Bernard's twisted corpse, Chant, the woman with the crimson-stained feather still in her hand. For a moment Chant was hopeful that the leader of the mercenaries would not understand Feather's part in what had happened, and she might still walk away. But it was not to be.

"Seize her," the Japanese commanded perfunctorily.

One of the black-uniformed men knocked the feather from the woman's hand, then gripped her tightly above the right elbow and led her out of the cell. Feather did not resist; once again, she seemed lost in the murky, midnight world from which she had emerged so briefly to save Chant's life.

Chant knew what would happen next, but there was nothing he could do to prevent it. While his man stepped to one side and aimed his submachine gun at Chant's knees, the tall Japanese stepped close to Chant.

"It is a pity that this must be your last battle, *Sensei,*" the man said, then struck Chant across the jaw with the butt of his Uzi.

TWENTY-ONE

HE AWOKE IN utter darkness, strapped firmly into the wheelchair. There was something very wrong, but it took him some time to identify exactly what it was that so particularly frightened him.

His jaw throbbed painfully, but as far as he could tell it was not broken. The fuzzy feeling in his head and the odd, metallic taste in his mouth told him that he had been drugged, and had been unconscious for an untold number of hours.

He was not in his cell; the stone room where he had been imprisoned had a particular smell to it, and it was not the smell of this place. This room smelled faintly medicinal, antiseptic.

And then it came to him—the most terrifying realization of all: he could not feel his legs. He was paralyzed from the waist down.

Despair and hopelessness threatened to pour out of his heart, and he struggled to contain it, taking deep breaths and marshaling his *kai* to suppress the panic. He was not dead yet, he thought—although he might well end up wishing he were. While he was unconscious, Richard Krowl could have taken away his legs forever with a single flick of his scalpel across the spinal cord.

If so, Chant thought, then he had surely lost. Without his legs, there was obviously no way for him to defeat Krowl and his remaining forces. There would be nothing left to do but defend himself with his last remaining weapon.

Lights slowly came up. As he had suspected, Chant found himself in the torture chamber. A clean linen sheet had been laid out over the operating table, and on the long stand next to it were an array of surgical instruments, including a power saw, and a stack of towels. In the dim light, he could see into the observation gallery above; the five remaining torturers were all seated in the front row. All were unshaven, unkempt, with drawn faces; but the eyes of every man glittered with excitement, and relief.

It was not difficult for Chant to see why. At the foot of the operating table, neatly arrayed on the white sheet, were his lock pick and the length of piano wire.

And so he was finished, Chant thought, and he began to go inside himself, searching for the proper balance of forces he would require to trigger his last weapon, a weapon which, to his knowledge, had not been used in centuries, and might only be a legend.

Footsteps came up behind him, stopped for a few seconds. Then Richard Krowl, wearing a green gown, shoe covers, and with a surgical mask draped around his neck, stepped around the chair to face Chant. He held Chant's dossier in his right hand.

"You did know Harry Gray, didn't you, Sinclair?"

Krowl asked in a soft voice. There was a hint of astonishment, even awe, in his voice. "He was a friend of yours. And the fact of the matter is that you allowed—maybe even set up—your capture in Amsterdam; you knew the CIA would try to break you, and when they couldn't, they'd send you here. My God, Sinclair, you *wanted* them to send you here. You *planned* on it. It's incredible. For you, this was just one more operation."

"I wouldn't exactly use that phrase," Chant said distantly, a faint smile on his face. He was deep into his mind now, searching, gathering together thoughts, focusing will. . . .

"Then it's true, isn't it?

"What have you done with the woman?"

Krowl rang the fingers of one hand through his long, blond hair, shook his head slightly. "You are indeed incredible. It turns out you're all the things people say you are—and more. Here you are locked up—*allowing* yourself to be locked up—during the day being tortured, and scampering around at night murdering my guards and guests, and otherwise taking care of your business affairs." Krowl paused, narrowed his lids. "Why didn't you kill us all the first night, Sinclair? I'm sure you could have. Why did you go back to your cell and take the chance that's now going to cost you so dearly?"

"I was having so much fun, I didn't want it to be over too quickly. I didn't know how long it would be before somebody flew over here looking for you, and I was afraid I might get bored."

"My apologies, gentlemen," Krowl announced to the torturers pressing up against the glass in the gallery. "I should have taken your warnings more seriously. I think you'll find that I'm about to more than make up for it—at least for the five of you who remain."

"What have you done with the woman?"

"How much do you care about her, Sinclair?"

"How much do *you* care about her?"

"I care enough not to torture her if you cooperate with me. I'll kill her now, because she's shown herself to be untrustworthy, but you can be assured that her death will be painless."

"You claim you're a researcher; you have no reason to hurt her."

"She killed Bernard."

"And did you a big favor. I thought you didn't torture people gratuitously."

"This wouldn't be gratuitous; it has a direct connection with you. I'm not going to bother with Cooked Goose for now, because you could still evade, and it would take too long to check out the information. There's time enough for that. However, you've hidden my records and the pearls somewhere on this island, and finding them could turn out to be a huge pain in the ass I don't need."

"And if I tell you where they are, you won't torture the woman?"

"Correct."

Chant told Krowl where to find the slipcovers.

"I believe you," Krowl said, and sighed. He gestured with his hand, and the last of Krowl's original guards, now dressed in a sterile surgical outfit, entered the room, stopped at the head of the operating table, next to a gas tank and a mask for administering anesthesia.

"So," Krowl continued, a slight note of regret in his voice, "now it's over for you. I hate to do this, because I still plan to explore your physical capabilities—to whatever extent possible. But you're far too dangerous to be allowed to walk around any longer. It's a shame to damage you as severely as I'm about to, but I now consider it absolutely essential."

Richard Krowl's voice now seemed very far away to

Chant, for Chant was very deep inside himself, near the source of his power.

"You've noticed, I'm sure, the lack of sensation below your waist. At the moment this is temporary, the result of a spinal injection. I'm afraid, though, that I'm going to have to amputate your legs, Mr. Sinclair, to make you a bit more manageable. . . ."

Now he had found the power, the sensations that had been spoken of. He gathered them together carefully, focused his will on them, shepherded them through his body until he felt a warm glow in the center of his body, just below his heart. He compressed the glow with his mind until it was a tiny pinpoint of energy that he could "see" as a shimmering point of light somewhere behind his eyes.

"So, you—or most of you—will still be going to Russia with me. We'll have long talks, you and I, about Cooked Goose, and other things. Can you hear me, John Sinclair?"

Ready.

"Put him on the table. I actually believe our fearsome *ninja* has fainted."

Chant was dimly aware of the steel cuffs on his wrists and ankles snapping free. Strong hands were gripping him under the arms, lifting him out of the chair and up onto the operating table.

Then Chant released the hold of his mind on the energy he had gathered and stored. The light inside his chest exploded, and he died.

TWENTY-TWO

"Damn it, he can't be dead! I never touched him!"

By tradition, the secret of *so-ka-meisei*—"warrior's merciful release"—was never written down, and the master who had instructed Chant had not known of anyone who had actually willed his own death, stopped heartbeat and respiration.

"Give me that syringe! No, not that one—that one!"

When Chant had begun his preparations, and then finally triggered the release of energy, he had fully expected to die. Of course, in a very real sense he was dead—clinically dead, with no vital signs. Krowl's panicked shouts and the fist pounding his chest attested to that. But what his teacher hadn't told him, and probably didn't know, was that consciousness obviously remained, at least for a short time.

"This son of a bitch did something to himself! Damn it, I won't let him cheat me like this! I won't let him die! Any vital signs yet?!"

"No, Doctor."

With his mind floating in this strange, uncharted land between life and death, Chant experienced no pain, and was at peace. He sensed that he had only to remain in this state for a little while longer, and he would drift off to . . . nothingness. Forever.

On the other hand . . .

"Keep pressing his chest! I have to check those instruments!"

Perhaps he could come back. He *felt* he could come back, simply by willing it. But why bother? What could he do? He was still paralyzed below the waist, laid out on an operating table, with two men hovering over him. He might not be able to enter into a state of *so-ka-meisei* again, which meant—

What the hell, Chant thought, and he opened his eyes to slits and released *kai* to his heart and lungs.

Krowl's assistant was beside his head, manipulating an oxygen mask and looking anxiously toward Krowl, who was standing a few feet away, preparing a syringe that Chant assumed was filled with adrenalin. With his peripheral vision, Chant could just see the top of the wheelchair next to the table, in line with his shoulders. Near his left-hand was the tray filled with surgical instruments.

A monitor beeped, and Chant abruptly sat up. Both Krowl and his assistant jumped, startled. In that instant, Chant grabbed a scalpel off the tray, whipped his hand back, and slit open the guard's throat. Blood sprayed over Chant and the table. Chant lunged for Krowl and missed as Krowl, eyes wide and mouth open, leaped back just in time.

"Get down here and help me!" Krowl screamed to the startled men in the gallery above him. "He can't go anywhere!"

As the torturers scrambled in the direction of a door to their left, Chant put the scalpel between his teeth, used his hands to push himself to the edge of the table, then off—into the wheelchair.

The force of his landing started the chair moving, but he was going in the wrong direction. He swiped with his right hand to make certain that the battery cables were disconnected, then came up with his fist underneath the tray of surgical instruments, sending them flying through the air toward the cowering Richard Krowl. Then Chant grasped the wheels of the chair, whipped himself around, and headed for Krowl's office. He sped through the office, into the long corridor.

There were the sounds of booted feet scrambling down a staircase to his left, twenty feet ahead. Chant took the scalpel in his left hand, held the blade out at a slight angle. A torturer stumbled breathless into the corridor, turned, and cried out as he saw Chant barreling toward him. The man leaped back toward the stairwell, colliding with two of his comrades, and Chant was just able to reach out with his scalpel and slash open the man's wrist. Chant barely got the scalpel back between his teeth before he smashed through the swinging doors at the end of the corridor and flew down the ramp outside, gaining speed.

All five mercenaries were outside, lounging on the grass under the bright moonlight, talking and laughing together while they smoked cigarettes and drank beer in the hot night. Their laughter abruptly stopped, turned to shouts of alarm and amazement as Chant, with a cursory wave, shot through and past them on the sidewalk leading to the helicopter pad.

He knew exactly where he wanted to go—the only place on the island he could go where there was any possibility, however slim, of escape.

Bullets started to whine around him, kicking off the concrete and whizzing past his head, as he reached the helicopter pad. Two bullets hit the back of the chair, but did not penetrate the steel back. Chant adjusted the direction of his wheelchair slightly as he crossed the pad, shot down the walk to the left. He was gaining speed all the time on the incline, and now he brought his arms in and rested his forearms on his lifeless thighs. He ducked his head and hunched his shoulders as more bullets caromed off the back of the wheelchair and the concrete.

Then the firing abruptly stopped, and there was only the sound of the whining rubber wheels and the wind in his ears as, still gaining speed, he approached the rim of the cliff overlooking the shark lagoon.

At the last moment he straightened up and firmly gripped the armrests of the wheelchair. Then he hit the rim of the cliff and soared off into space, fell through night toward the blue-black, glassy surface of the water far below, and the silent death beneath it.

He knew he would break his back if he hit the water the wrong way, and so, still holding the wheelchair firmly to his body, he rolled in space, spinning lazily over and over, maneuvering to land the safest way—head first. He did so, and the headrest of the wheelchair absorbed some of the shock of entry. Still, the force of concussion was enough to tear the coveralls off his torso and rip open his belly and shoulder wounds. Blood, even darker than the moonlit water, swirled about him, and an instant later even darker shapes began to move about him. Then his shoulder brushed against the sandy bottom.

Chant released his grip on the wheelchair with his right hand and took the scalpel from his mouth. At the same time he used his left hand to hold the chair over him, providing a partial shield against the sharks, which now seemed to be everywhere, circling and darting in, their razor teeth gnashing on, shaking, the steel chair. Chant crouched on the bottom beneath the chair, then thrust out his right hand as one of the dark shapes flashed by. The scalpel caught the shark just beneath the jaw, penetrated the tough, leathery skin. The force of the shark's passage ripped the scalpel from Chant's hand, but not before the razor-sharp blade had torn open the shark's belly. Blood and viscera dropped into the water, totally obscuring Chant's vision. Still he crouched on the bottom, bracing the wheelchair over his head as the sharks went into a feeding frenzy.

His lungs were beginning to ache.

He'd certainly provided a spectacular show for anybody watching from the top of the cliff, Chant thought, and now it was time for him to make a graceful exit—if he could. He still had a way to go.

He estimated that he had been under water less than a minute. Under normal conditions, he could hold his breath for close to three and a half minutes, but he did not have to remind himself that cowering under a wheelchair in the midst of a shark feeding frenzy while an anxious audience watched on from above was not exactly a normal condition.

But he badly—very badly—wanted to see Dr. Richard Krowl's face one more time.

With no feeling or power in his legs, Chant knew that trying to drag the chair after him would expend too much energy. He released his grip on it, turned on his belly, dug his fingers into the sandy bottom and pulled himself through the cloud of dark blood, angling slightly to his right. There was tremendous movement in the water as the creatures just above his head slashed at each other, but, as he'd hoped, they seemed too busy at the moment feeding on each other to notice him.

Again, he knew exactly where he wanted to go, and if he had not lost his sense of direction under the water, that was where he was heading—the underwater caves at the northern end of the lagoon where Bernard had gathered the pearl-bearing oysters. With luck, whatever one he entered would have some kind of space above the waterline.

With a great deal of luck. But Chant knew that he had no choice but to enter one of the caves, for to try to surface through the feeding sharks would be to almost surely die, if not from the teeth of the sharks, then finally at the hands of the men he knew had to be looking down from atop the cliff.

With his lifeless legs dragging after him in the sand, Chant pulled with powerful strokes, streamlining his body after each stroke to minimize water resistance and knifing through the bloody darkness. The ache in his lungs became a burning sensation. He desperately needed to breathe, and the urge to try to make the surface was almost overwhelming. But he resisted it, kept pulling. Something heavy and rough scraped across his back—but there was no rending of teeth, and even if a shark had torn a chunk off one of his paralyzed legs, he knew he would have felt the terrible tug. He kept going.

Pull, glide . . . *pull,* glide . . . He concentrated on the rhythm of his strokes, occasionally blowing a few bubbles to ease the pressure on his lungs, suppressing oxygen-burning panic. *Pull,* glide . . . *pull,* glide . . .

Suddenly he emerged from the cloud of blood into clear water. Two black shapes veered down at him from above. Chant hugged the bottom, pressing his body against the sand, and the shapes darted away to disappear into the cloud of blood behind him.

Pull, glide . . . *pull,* glide.

Was he heading in the right direction? Perhaps he had misjudged, Chant thought, and was heading out into the middle of the lagoon or toward the sea. Should he surface? One gulp of air, even if it were his last, would taste so good. . . .

Pull, glide . . . *pull,* glide.

He couldn't hold out much longer, Chant thought. He estimated that he had been under water well over two minutes now, and his chest felt as if it were about to explode from the pressure of poisonous air. He released more bubbles.

Pull, glide . . . *pull,* glide.

No more, Chant thought; even if he were heading in the right direction, he couldn't make it. He felt himself on the verge of passing out, and it seemed senseless to drown when he might have at least *some* chance on the surface. He was about to head up when two jet-black holes suddenly loomed a few yards away from him.

The mouths of caves.

He had come this far . . .

Pull, glide . . . *pull,* glide.

Once he entered a cave, Chant thought, he would no longer have any option. If there was no opening to the surface, he would die under black water, clawing at rock. If he died, Feather, the men in the shacks, and the broken people died with him. The Petroffs would die, or fervently wish they were dead.

Surface, or enter a cave?

Three sharks made his decision for him, and Chant pulled himself into the black mouth of a cave just as they passed through the space where he had been a moment before.

He released more air, knew that he had only a few more seconds of consciousness left. He rolled over on his back, reached up and grabbed the rough stone just a few inches away from his face and began to pull hand-over-hand.

Pull! Pull! Pull!

He was finished, Chant thought. He couldn't go on any longer. Any moment now he would either pass out, or the air would burst from his lungs and he would involuntarily suck in—water.

Pull!

Still he kept going, feeling the skin tear away from his palms and fingers. Then, as he reached up with his right hand for what he was certain would be his last pull, his hand missed rock, broke the surface of the water into—air.

Chant surfaced with a great, barking explosion of air from his lungs. Panting, gasping for breath, he floundered in the water, only vaguely aware of what looked like the moon high above his head, as if glimpsed through a telescope. He continued to flounder as he gasped the sweet, fresh air. Then the knuckles of his right hand bounced painfully off a rough edge. He explored the surface with his hands, found it to be the lip of a narrow rock shelf. With his last strength, he dragged himself up out of the water onto the shelf. Then he collapsed to the stone and passed out.

TWENTY-THREE

WHEN HE AWOKE, the sky at the top of the natural stone chimney above his head was barely aglow with a murky, misty dawn. Unless he had lost track of time, Chant thought, it was the day the Petroffs were to be brought to the island. At most, he might have a few hours. . . .

Feeling had returned to his lower body, but he was very weak. He raised himself to his hands and knees, stayed in that position a few moments until his head stopped reeling. The air wafting down through the chimney smelled of rain, and he felt chilled and clammy.

If it were misty and raining, Chant thought, the helicopter might not come. There was no way of knowing.

He slowly rose to his feet, swayed slightly, then went through a series of exercises to increase his blood flow and flex his stiff muscles. He knew he was near the end of his resources, and from somewhere deep inside himself he was going to have to summon up sufficient strength and will to finish the task he had set for himself.

He sat down on the stone shelf, used his herb-hardened nail to open the callus under his left heel, where there was a second small packet of the herb mixture that once before had served him so well. He opened the packet, put the green mixture in his mouth and chewed slowly. Within thirty seconds his head cleared, and he could feel strength returning to his arms and legs. His heart fluttered dangerously, but then settled into a strong, slightly heightened beat. He licked condensation off the rock walls to slake his terrible thirst, took a series of deep breaths to focus his *kai,* then slowly but steadily began to climb up the rock chimney toward the gray sky.

"Yield or die," Chant said softly.

The tall Japanese, his Uzi slung over his shoulder, had been standing near the edge of the cliff, smoking a cigarette and staring out at the fog-shrouded sea. The man dropped the cigarette, wheeled. He started to reach for his gun, then froze when he saw the tall figure in stained, tattered coveralls standing before him. A look of astonishment passed over his face, and then he smiled thinly.

"Welcome back from the dead, *Sensei,*" the Japanese replied evenly. He straightened up from his crouch—but did not take his hands away from his gun. "Somehow, I find I'm not that surprised to see you. How did you manage—?"

"Yield or die," Chant repeated. "Your skills and weapons are for hire, and you've done your job. The man who hired you is now as good as dead; you and your men cannot protect him."

"I understand . . . and I believe that what you say is true.

Unless, of course, I manage to shoot you now. Considering your condition, it might have been better if you'd shoved me off the cliff."

"I know my condition, so it becomes something for you to consider. If you believe you can kill me before I kill you, then you may wish to try. Then you will die. I suggest that Dr. Krowl and the men he has brought here are not good people to die for."

"You must be very weak now."

"Decide now," Chant said curtly.

The Japanese studied Chant for some time, then very slowly unslung the submachine gun and handed it to Chant, butt first. "I yield, *Sensei,*" he said quietly.

Chant broke open the magazine and examined it; it was full. "Will you work for me?" he asked as he snapped the magazine back into the stock.

"I would consider it an honor, *Sensei,*" the Japanese answered with a slight bow.

"What's your name?"

"Akiro."

"What about your men? Will they come over to me?"

Akiro shrugged. "I will find out."

"I want only men I can trust, as I now trust you."

"I understand, *Sensei*. And I thank you. I will make my selection carefully."

"I need this gun. Can you get another from one of your men?"

"Yes."

"Has Krowl sent anyone to search in the brush around the complex?"

"Not that I know of, *Sensei*—and I would know." He paused, smiled thinly. "Whatever you've hidden is still there."

Chant grunted. "It stands to reason; he was waiting for you people to leave. There are pearls. I will share them with you and any of your men who will work for me."

"I do not require payment from you, *Sensei*. Watching you work, and now working with you, is a lesson of very great value. You are even more powerful than the legends indicate."

"Well, I'm still alive," Chant said with a shrug. "But we will share the pearls." He paused, smiled wryly. "I don't work for nothing; neither shall you."

"As you wish, *Sensei*."

"Where's the woman?"

"Krowl gave her to his . . . guests . . . for their use." The Japanese seemed embarrassed. "I believe she's still in their building."

So much for the torture doctor's word, Chant thought as he abruptly slung the Uzi over his shoulder. "Where's Krowl?"

"I saw him walking by himself earlier, but I believe he went to his office."

"He's up early."

"He's upset because he thinks he lost you to the sharks. He'd bragged to us about how you were going to teach him the secrets of the *ninja* while he dragged you around behind him on a cart."

"Did a helicopter land yesterday or this morning?"

"No, *Sensei*."

"Is one scheduled to land today?"

"I don't know. Unless it clears, I'm not sure one could land today."

A potential problem, Chant thought, but there was nothing to be done about it. "If and when that helicopter lands, you'll really start earning your pay. I'm almost certain there'll be armed men on board; I don't know how many, but they'll be very good. Obviously, I want that helicopter, but there'll be a couple on board and I want every precaution taken to make certain they aren't harmed."

"I understand, *Sensei.*"

"I'll take care of Krowl and the torturers. You talk to your men and see who's willing to work with us; if you have to do any killing, try to do it quietly. I don't want Krowl to suspect anything's wrong until I have my hands on him."

"I understand, *Sensei.*"

"After you've selected your men, free the men in the shacks down by the shark lagoon, as well as any other prisoners around here I don't know about."

"I don't believe there are any."

"Well, check it out—quietly. Then round up all the broken people you find wandering around here. Take everybody to the cellblock and wait. I'll join you there when I've taken care of my business."

"Good hunting, *Sensei,*" the tall Japanese said quietly as Chant melted away into the mist.

Richard Krowl was not in his office, nor did Chant find him in the adjoining cottage. Unwilling to risk the possibility of Krowl discovering what was happening and getting to the radio before he did, Chant decided to take a calculated risk of his own. He went to the radio shack and, using a special, ultrahigh frequency, sent out a series of coded messages that Gerard Patreaux would be waiting for; the machinery for medical attention, forged documents, and covert transportation would be set in motion. Then Chant removed a key component from the radio, put it in his pocket, and went next door to the dormitory.

He found Feather tied to a bedpost in a room on the first floor. Her hair was disheveled, but she was dressed and did not appear to be harmed. She looked up, saw him standing in the doorway, and her face lit up with joy. Tears welled in her eyes.

Chant put his finger to his lips, then mouthed the words: "Are you all right?"

Feather nodded her head. Chant stepped into the bedroom and perfunctorily snapped the neck of the man sleeping in the bed. He untied the weeping woman, held her in his arms for a few moments, then gently removed her arms from around his neck and motioned for her to stand behind the door. "I'll be right back," he said, and left the room.

He found his second victim in the bathroom, shaving, and Chant quietly slit his throat.

As he started up to the second floor, a man appeared at the head of the stairwell. The man shrieked when he saw Chant, turned to run. With the silence already broken and the radio disabled, Chant was no longer as concerned as he had been with silent killing; he snapped the Uzi into firing position and pulled the trigger, blowing the man's head off with one burst.

He machine-gunned the last two remaining torturers as they rushed from their rooms into the hall, then once again slung the smoking submachine gun over his shoulder and returned to Feather.

"Let's go, Maria," Chant said, taking the woman's hand and leading her from the room. "Everyone who should be safe is. You're going to be all right. As soon as I find the good doctor and put him on ice, we're all going to have ourselves one hell of a picnic while we wait for some visitors. I'm just a bit hungry."

With Feather hugging him around the waist and leaning on him, Chant went down the corridor to the entrance—where he abruptly stopped, then quickly stepped back as he pushed Feather behind him.

Outside, on the rectangle of concrete a hundred yards away, a huge Russian military helicopter sat, its rotors still running.

State-of-the-art radar and equipped for silent running,

Chant thought. The Russians would be on a tight schedule in this part of the world, and the fog had not deterred them. He had not heard the rotors over the sound of the machine-gun fire; he could only hope they had not heard the machine-gun fire over the sound of their rotors.

Regardless of what they had heard, the Russians were obviously suspicious. While the rotors continued to turn, two men in civilian clothes and with the unmistakable mien of KGB descended from the cargo bay door, heavy machine guns held ready. The men slowly spread apart twenty yards, looked around them at the deserted complex.

Where was Krowl?!

"Take this," Chant said, shoving the Uzi into the woman's hands. "No matter what happens out there, don't use it—except to defend yourself. I don't think that will happen, because those men will just go away if there's an . . . incident. If anything happens to me—"

"Please don't die, John Sinclair," the woman said clearly.

Chant smiled, kissed her on the forehead, then removed the radio component from his pocket and gave it to her. "If anything happens to me, hide for as long as you need to, then try to get to the cellblock. That's where the others are. Give that transistor to the tall Japanese. He'll know what to do with it, and there must be people he can contact who will come for you. I believe he can be trusted."

"Please don't die, John Sinclair," she said. "You are all I have to hang on to."

"Tell him he'll find his pearls buried behind the first line of brush, about ten yards due north of the center of the helicopter pad. Say he'll earn his pay by making sure you and the others are protected and cared for. After he gets you off this island and someplace safe, he must contact Gerard Patreaux, who's head of Amnesty, Inc. in Geneva. When Patreaux has arranged for the transfer of all of you to his care, the Japanese's job will be finished. Will you remember?"

"Let the helicopter go. Another will come when the weather clears."

"I can't do that, Maria," Chant said, and he stepped out into the misty morning.

The KGB men immediately caught his movement, swung the barrels of their heavy machine guns in his direction.

Chant, very conscious of his tattered clothes, raised both hands into the air and waved. "Good morning!" he called cheerily in Russian. "Hey, we were afraid you weren't going to make it in this soup! Come on in the building; there's plenty of hot coffee!"

"Stop!" the man on the right commanded in Russian. "Where is everyone?! Why wasn't our radio communication answered?!"

He'd covered thirty yards, seventy to go. Chant kept walking. "One of the men fell into a hole back there in the brush, and it's taking all of us to get him out. Relax! Come and have some coffee!" Fifty yards to go. "Dr. Krowl and the others will be here in a few minutes, and we'll all have breakfast!"

"I told you to stop!" the man shouted, and fired a burst, expertly aimed, that kicked up chunks of concrete to either side of Chant. Chant stopped. "Identify yourself! We were told nobody on the island spoke Russian!"

Oh-oh, Chant thought. He was trying to think of some response when Richard Krowl suddenly burst from behind the windowless building and sprinted toward the helicopter.

"Help me!" Krowl shouted. "You have to take me off this—!"

Startled, the KGB man on the left swung around and pressed the trigger of his machine gun. Slugs tore into

Richard Krowl's legs. He screamed in agony, flew through the air, and landed in a crumpled heap.

As soon as the first guard had turned, Chant had started to sprint toward the brush to his right. He did not think he could make it before the KGB men gunned him down, but he felt it was his only chance. Out of the corner of his eye he saw both men swing their guns toward him—and then the man on the left was blown away by a hail of machine-gun fire that came from the direction of the complex. The second man immediately dropped to his belly and began returning the fire. Chant dived the remaining few feet, landed in the brush, and rolled to his right, toward the thorn bush where he had hidden one of the brown-uniformed guard's guns. He crawled on his belly the last few remaining yards, reached into the heart of the bush—and grasped the gun.

When he peered over the top of the brush, he could see the KGB man, with his heavy-caliber machine gun, pinning down Akiro and his men—and Feather—with withering bursts of fire. Two of the mercenaries lay in pools of blood on the ground.

Then the helicopter began to lift off the ground, leaving the KGB man behind. . . .

Chant suddenly leapt to his feet, aimed the gun with both hands, and put a single round through the KGB agent's forehead. Then he tossed the gun away, leapt over the bush, and sprinted through a cloud of dust toward the helicopter.

The pilot saw him, and began veering away from Chant and heading toward the edge of the escarpment. Arms and legs pumping, breath rasping in his lungs, Chant raced after the helicopter. He did not hesitate at the edge of the cliff, and flung himself out into space, reaching with extended arms toward the open cargo bay. His fingers caught the edge of the bay, gripped, and Chant swung beneath the craft, banging painfully against its underside. For a few moments he twisted and swung out of control—but he hung on.

The pilot, perhaps sensing the shift in weight, began a series of defensive maneuvers, swooping and wheeling in an attempt to shake Chant off; when that failed, he tried scraping him off.

For the moment, Chant could do nothing but hang on as the helicopter banked sharply and came in close to the face of the escarpment. Below him, Chant could see the survivors of Torture Island—Akiro and two of his mercenaries, Feather, the white-haired broken people—staring up at him. Feather stood with her arms outstretched, as if to catch him if he fell.

Only two faces were not turned up toward him. Richard Krowl was frantically dragging himself and his bloody, shattered legs along the ground in an apparent attempt to get away from a man dressed all in white. Suddenly the broken man rushed at Krowl, pushed the torture doctor to the ground, and began slamming his head against it. As high in the air as he was, Chant could still hear Krowl's agonizing shriek as the crazed flesh-eater lowered his head toward Krowl's neck, and began to tear the flesh with his teeth.

Then the helicopter banked out toward sea. This time Chant timed the swaying of his body so that at the apogee of a swing he was able to hook his ankle over the edge of the bay door. In moments he was over the edge and into the bay, steadying himself by gripping the edges of two bunks that had been anchored to the floor. Strapped into the bunks, unconscious and obviously drugged, were an elderly man and woman. Viktor and Olga Petroff.

The wide-eyed Russian pilot had a pistol in his hand, but he was strapped into his seat and it was difficult for him to pilot the basically unstable craft, turn around, and fire at the same time. He did manage to get off one wild shot that went through the ceiling before Chant darted forward, ripped the gun from his grasp, and stuck the barrel into the pilot's ear.

"Come on, comrade," Chant shouted above the chopper noise. "You don't want me to put a big bullet in your brain, do you? Now be a good Russian and put this fucking thing on the ground. I have a pick-up to make."